CW00832600

WHEN ENGLAND SANK

WHEN ENGLAND SANK

Leah Renai Gee

Book Guild Publishing
Sussex, England

First published in Great Britain in 2010 by
The Book Guild Ltd
Pavilion View
19 New Road
Brighton, BN1 1UF

Typesetting in Garamond by Ellipsis Books Ltd, Glasgow

Printed in Great Britain by CPI Antony Rowe

A catalogue record for this book is available from The British Library.

ISBN 978 1 84624 503 9

This book is dedicated to my father,
George – with thanks for his unwavering wisdom,
his warm words and his constant love.

'In man's analysis and understanding of himself, it is as well to know where he came as whither he is going.'

Edgar Cayce

Preface

What is England?

Armada, architecture, art deco, archbishop, Austen, alliances, America's lapdog (*a global joke really*), autism, anorexic super-models, anorexic girls, accountability, accounts, academies, Andrew Lloyd Webber, abortions, asylum seekers, ASBOs, athe-ists, auction sites, alternative therapies, Anfield, Angel of the North, the Ashes, ashtrays, allotments, Attenborough, arcades, Ascot, Alan Partridge, after-school clubs. Breakfast clubs, Boudicca, Battle of Bosworth, beefeaters, 'Britannia rule (*not 'rules'*) the waves!', Buckingham Palace, baroque grandeur, best china for our guests, Brontë sisters, Black Penny stamps, bowler hats, Bank Holiday weekends, ballroom, Big Ben, broadsheets, briefcases, biros, the British pound, Brit pop, the Blitz, bonuses, Bluewater, Buddha ornaments, Buster, business class (*we can live in hope*), benefits, benefit cheats, Bobby Moore, beetles, the Beatles, BMWs, BMXs, the BBC, boarding schools, bulimia, breast enlargements, breast reductions, botox, barbecues in the rain, Blackpool, binge drinking, the British bulldog, British beef, battery hens, butchers, bakeries, barbers, black cabs, bus lanes, bus lane fines, Butlins, Big Brother, BNP, brownies, Beckham, butter, buttercups. Carnations, culture, castles, chess, Christianity, Catholicism, Church of England, churches,

Cathedrals (*so spectacular!*), choirs, choristers, Charles, Civil War, coronation, Coronation Street, coronation chicken, chicken tikka vindaloo, colonialism, Commonwealth, the Channel, channel swimmers, croquet, crosswords, Chelsea Flower Show, conkers, conscientious objectors, Cat Stevens, crown jewels, corgis, Churchill (*a cool puff of superiority and wisdom*), Constable, countryside (*gorgeous landscapes*), cottages, caravans, Cornwall, Cleveland, Chester, comprehensives, Conservatives, Cambridge, catchment areas, Carnaby Street, celebrity, consumerism, commercialism, Christmas, circuses, Concorde, cities, cycling, camping, chavs, council housing, council tax, car tax, chlamydia, clap clinics, contraceptive pills, cups of tea, cottage pie, cheddar, cheesy music, Cluedo, childcare, cafes, chip butties, chips and gravy (*only in the North!*), cod, cigarettes, cigars, charlie, Celtic scorn (*and countless countries' loathing*), cinema, Carry On England. Drake, Darcy, dragon-slayers, damsels in distress, duels, Disraeli, democracy, Dickens' magical ink, dyslexia, dyspraxia, Daley Thompson, Downing Street, debt (*a country running itself on debt*), designer labels only, delays, divorce, dress-down Friday, drive on the left, disrespecting youths (*who disrespect pensioners*), dealers, dialects, Dizzee Rascal, darts, dunking biscuits, daisies, daisy chains, digital televisions, degrees, data, Diana. English Rose, Eliza Doolittle, Earth is flat, Earth is round, Empire's eyes, London Eye, escalators, Edward Burne-Jones, Emin, equal opportunities, education for all, Eton for a select few, emigration, evacuees, environment, epidemics, essential oils, European Union, expenses scandals, eastenders, e-numbers, Elton John, en suites, ecstasy. Faustus, Forster, the Falklands War, free-range, farms, fishmongers, February snow (*two inches deep, yet it halts a nation*), foxes, foxhunting, fencing, the four-minute mile, flags, fags, football fans (*causing havoc abroad*), FA Cup Final, football-loathing girlfriends, fake tans, freckles, fry-ups, fridge magnets, feminists, fashion, front doors *('you used to be able to leave your front door open all day long … but not any more!')*, ferries, a Fat Controller, fat policemen, five a day, French and Saunders, Facebook, films, flatscreens, four-dimensional scans, the Footsie Index, funfairs, Folkestone races. Gregorian monks chanting, the Golden Age, Guy Fawkes, the Globe, the Grand Exhibition, gardens, the Gherkin Building, ghurkas, gypsies, general elections, a gormless Government, gambling, greyhound races, the Grand National, the grammar school system, grammatical errors, Greenwich meantime, Geordies, Gazza's tears, Glastonbury, gang culture, games consoles, gadgets *(all sorts!)*, gluttony, GCSEs, G-A-Y Bar, girls' nights out, a glass half full, a glass half empty, gin and tonic *(on the rocks)*. History, Hillsborough disaster, health and safety, health shops, health farms, harvests, hosepipe bans, hangings, Heathcliff, hobbits, Hogwarts, Harry Potter, headlice, headlines, 'Harry Patch dies at the age of 111', Holst, Henry Cooper, Houses of Parliament, Hung Parliament, HRH, Heathrow, Hugh Grant *(always the same!)*, hoodies, hairdressers, hayfever, half sisters, half brothers, hopscotch. The Iron Age, the Industrial Revolution, immigration, intoxicated teenagers *(nothing better to do)*, illiterate youngsters, Iraq, innocent soldiers, interest rates, the Independent. Jesters, James Bond, Joan Collins, jabs, Jags, Jamie Oliver, job centres. Knights of the Round Table, knighthoods, Kitchener's convincing eyes, Kate Moss, 'kiss me quick' hats, karaoke, ketchup, kite-flying. D. H. Lawrence, Laurence Olivier, Lady with the Lamp, locomotives, low-cost airlines, Liberal Democrats, Labour, local government, Lenny Henry, lavender, lager, lager, more lager, lung cancer, litter, loans, lion … a British Lion, the lads, lawyers, legal aid, LFC, the London Marathon, Linford Christie, London 2012, Lewis Hamilton, landlines, laptops. Merlin, Martello towers, the Magna Carta,

Marlowe, Moseley, a magical wardrobe, miners, the miners' strike, Mini-coopers, mini-breaks, Matthew Street, Morecambe and Wise, Michael Caine, multi-culturalism, Muslims, Marmite, mushy peas, mayonnaise, Monopoly, mortgages, motorways, M20, MI5, the Midlands, the Millenium Dome, museums, music in Manchester, Man U, Ministry of Sound, morning after pills, mobiles, more and more millionaires, more and more meditation classes. Nineteen sixty-six (*the eternal victory*), 1984, nursery rhymes, never will win Wimbledon again, Number 10, the National Health Service, nine 'til five, nice glass of wine in the evening, nail technicians, nightclubs, networking, the Navy, the news. Oscar Wilde (*despite being Dublin-born!*), opera, Oxford, the Oval, overpaid footballers, overworked teachers, overcrowded hospitals, overdoses, overtime, orderly queues of one, one-way systems, obesity, Operation Stack, oak trees, organic products, optimism. Pessimism, pesticides, Princes in the Tower, Prince Albert's thoughtless comments, *Paradise Lost*, pollution, penny farthings, pocket watches, 'Please Sir. Can I have some more?', pineapple and cheese sticks, Poppins, poppies, pantomimes, pigtails, pigeons, pheasants, pine, part of the United Kingdom, part of Great Britain, part of the European Union, Pratchett, propaganda, punk, Philharmonic Orchestra, pit bulls, push-up bras, Page 3 Girls, power showers, pilates, pensions, prescription drugs, painkillers, Proms, premiers, the Premiership, pubs, pot, polytechnics, paedophiles, poll tax, parking tickets, petrol, puddles, pebbles, pornography, Prime Minister's question time, property, property development, public hangings, Protestant witch? Queen Elizabeth I (*standing on her globe of the world. Legend has it that her skin, heavily clad in thick white make-up, had maggots breeding underneath it. Crawling. Could she not feel that? Queasiness.*), questionable sentencing, quills, qwerty. Rain, rain and more rain (*we never cease to be surprised by the rain*), 'Ring a Ring o' Roses', rapeseed, Renaissance, Raleigh, Royal Mint, Royal Ballet, Royal Bank of England, registry offices, the RAF, recession, Rover, rising fuel costs, referendums, red buses, Rolling Stones, a retro style, rustic public houses, renovations, roast dinners, ready salted crisps, roses, ribbons, rugby (*union and league*), reality TV, Rooney, Ricky Gervais, Rowling, risk assessments, Robin Hood. Sheriff of Nottingham, St. George, The Sword in the Stone, Stonehenge, Spiritualism, six wives, Spenser, stained-glass windows, Shakespeare's almighty playscripts, smugglers, suffragettes, scones, strawberries and cream, summer holidays, Seasonal Affective Disorder, sparrows, Stock Exchange, sewage, sirens, students (*and how infuriating students can be!*), student debt, SATs, school photos, sex education at five, STDs, single mums, Shagaloof, supermarket giants, soap operas, the Square Mile, 'shaken, not stirred', Simon Cowell, seascapes, seaside holidays, southerners (*still a target for Northern resentment*), the Spice Girls break America, the scouse sense of humour, speed dating, sunburn (*consistently takes us by surprise, year on year*), skin cancer, sushi, sudoko, scouts, 'snap!', snakes and ladders, second homes abroad, sensors, Stephen Hawking, Science unbounded ... (*out of control*), superbugs, supplements, spies, smack, smoking, smoking ban, security cameras, sunsets, Sky One, satellites, sarcasm, sleeze. Toilet humour, the Tower, 'That's cricket!', Turner, tractors, trilby hats, top hats, tweed, tradition, teddy bears' picnics, the theatre, trams, towns, the Tunnel, the Thames, the Trent, trains, Thatcher, thatched roofs, taxes, trade unions, the Treasury, technology, two point four children, the Territorial Army, terrorism creeping in, teenage stabbings, teenage pregnancies, tummy tucks, tattoos, tabloids, Take That, targets, too much testing, trout, tartare sauce, the three lions. Unsuccessful penalty shoot-outs, under-aged mothers, the underground ...

(*the mind-numbing underground*), umbrellas, universities, university of life, underachieving graduates, unknown soldiers. Villages, Victoria, Vivien Leigh, Virginia Woolf, vintage, vases, Valentine's Day (*over-hyped*), veterans (*forgotten figures*), victims, vodka, veneers, Vera Lynn. White Cliffs, the Warren, William the Conqueror, Wordsworth, workhouses, World Wars, war heroes, wireless networks, Wi-Fi, the West End, the Welfare State, waiting lists, white-collar workers, Wembley, WAGs, Winehouse, worms being flung about in the January winds, water features, winter (*as Byron states, 'ending in July, to recommence in August'.*) The X-factor, x-rated material (*abundantly available.*) Yew trees, yucca plants, youth, young offenders, yobs, yoga, yo-yos, yesterday ... oh and, last, but certainly not least, Ziggy Stardust!

This is England as I know it.

Modern life. It is achieving what is regarded as 'success' but, in reality, with modern life, there do arise all the problems that spoil our life experience. It is this 'success' that masks these problems. False values are always transient, and material life will always be in turmoil. Why is this so? Because the Soul lives on in non-material planes ... its natural habitat. This is the enigma of human choice.

Part One

1

We are all in the gutter, but some of us are looking at the stars.
                                                    Oscar Wilde

Everyday a hardworking fisherman rows his boat to sea. He is an honest man, who leads an honest life. His son accompanies him each day and, together, the two men haul the nets in optimistically. If the nets are abundantly full, they laugh together joyfully. If the nets are empty, they make every effort to keep one another's spirits up, by cracking a joke or by whistling an uplifting tune. However, they both experience the weight of each other's growing sadness and anxiety.

Both men lead consistently simple and dignified lives, and, as they talk amongst the waves, they both look back affectionately towards the land. They always have done. The harbour, the cliff, the pier, the fish market. They both know the landscape intimately – as well as they know each other's sun-kissed, innocent freckles.

Therefore, both men notice that the formerly regal, white cliff now appears rapidly shrunken. OVERNIGHT.

Therefore, both men notice that the large, dressed rocks that make up the pier have suddenly diminished in number. No one else notices.

Therefore, both men feel a growing sadness and anxiety:

they instinctively feel that some kind of incomprehensible tragedy is about to take place … the land screams this out to them. When they tell people this, they are merely laughed at. Scorn's face.

One day a hardworking fisherman and his son sail out to sea, never to dock again. Only the memory of the lost landscape – which is imprinted in their hearts – remains. It remains forever. They never look back. They never look back at what is left behind. Why would they? They only look forwards now, to the future. They slowly begin to find comfort and joy in each other's company once again.

2

Words are easy, like the wind;
Faithful friends are hard to find.
William Shakespeare

It was a bright September day when the US President received the phone call. He dropped the phone without reply … The land of England, Scotland and Wales – Great Britain – was sinking, and it was sinking fast. Within three months, it would have completely disappeared under the sea. The President called an emergency meeting in order to decide the fate of the island's 60 million inhabitants.

All world leaders dropped what they were doing to attend this meeting, which was to be held in Washington, the very next day.

'I have an announcement. Something is about to occur – the magnitude of which is beyond all human comprehension. And, yet, we must take the reins and try to carry out the necessary measures to cope. We are here today to urgently decide what is to be the fate of the British citizens, for, within three to four months, the land will have gone under water. It will be gone. Completely gone. It will be no more.

'The English fishing community first made mention of this freak occurrence some months ago, but only now have geological experts – (without exception, I may add) – confirmed its inevitability. Lady, gentlemen: a globo-socio-econo-geo-politico disaster awaits us!'

SILENCE.

Then, all of a sudden, a state of tornado-like confusion rapidly burst through the Council. Some leaders cried out; some leaders, virgins to tears, wept for the first time; some leaders tried to dispel the smirks that were satanically creeping onto their fat, sweaty cheeks.

'What will we do?'

'How do we deal with this?'

'Where will the people go?'

'Can't we just leave them? ... Let's just leave them to dr-own!' (*The latter word was extended to two syllables, and was also accompanied by a thick shower of saliva, for dramatic effect.*)

A few minutes passed, which allowed the initial announcement to solidify in the minds of the Council Members. The cries gradually began to die down as the crimson-faced participants came to their senses; for their one consolation was that the most powerful man in the world, the man that they, without exception, all looked up to, always sounded so strong, always sounded so authoritative, always sounded so knowing ... always sounded so powerful. His calming aura radiated around the huge hall reaching everybody. It reached into every corner.

'What can we do to help, Mr President?'

SILENCE.

' ... Mr President?'

SILENCE.

'I don't know, I really don't know!' whined the President in a childlike way. His body withered suddenly.

The following day, the floral-embodied first lady was flown

in. She, rather abruptly, slapped her husband across the face, in order to bring him to his senses once more. Following this momentary hiccup, some conclusions quickly (and rather haphazardly) began to be formulated regarding the future of the British citizens.

3

Extract from the Prime Minister's Speech to the Nation, 6 October 2013, 06:00 hours.

'I am here today to talk to the people of England, Scotland and Wales. I am here, not to address the nation as its leader, but to reach each person as a true friend. For, we are all the same person now: men, women, children, soldiers, city workers, students, asylum seekers, people of Afro-Caribbean descent, people of Eastern European descent – we all melt into one vicious, inhumane furnace.

'I will not be able to hide the terrible truth from you, for you are an intelligent people. I cannot soften the painful blows, or lighten these menacing words. People of our nation ... within three months the land of Great Britain will have sunk. Sunk forever. (*NB The speech was delayed at this point, for the crescendo of reporters' gasps, cries and shouts lasted several agonising minutes.*)

'Leading experts say there is nothing we can do to stop this incomprehensible tragedy. There is nothing we can do to even slow it down. However, we must always remember that, where the land perishes, its people must blossom. A mass evacuation of all people will take place with immediate effect. Residents of Wales will be transported to Australia. Residents of Scotland will be transported to Russia. Irish-born citizens will return to their homeland.

PAUSE.

' ... Residents of England will be transported to ... to various countries around the world *(a guilty cough)*. Where possible, families will travel together, by air and by boat. Each person will shortly receive details regarding their newly designated country of residence, as well as compulsory instructions to follow in preparation for that journey ...'

The Prime Minister left the press conference sweating. This was 'the prime minister without a personality' ... yet his heart was racing fast. He answered none of the questions that flew violently at him. He did not even hear them. He had only one thing on his mind. One thing he had to do immediately ...

He was protected by four sturdy, clone-like bodyguards as he made his way to the awaiting black car. The car somehow fought its way through the tirade of questions and the flashing of cameras, and then, skidding, sped off around the corner. A traffic jam had already formed on the main road due to this newborn national state of confusion. The Prime Minister, therefore, did not reach his destination for several hours. He felt annoyed, for never was his time more precious than in this moment. When he did finally arrive at Number 10, he did not greet his family *(though they had so wanted to console the 'iron man')*. Instead, he immediately went to his office, slammed the door shut, and took large, confident strides towards his elaborately baroque desk, where he personally dialled the number to reach the White House. This call was *strictly* confidential.

'Hello. It's the Prime Minister of Great Britain,' he said quickly. (Traces of an aristocratic heritage were firmly clamped to the tones of his voice, despite the haphazard speed with which the disturbed leader had delivered the sentence.)

'I need to speak to the President immediately ... yes, yes, yes – it is an emergency ...'

Two-and-a-half minutes later, the British leader had begun his lifeline conversation with the US President.

'Mr President, I need to ask a great favour of you: in exchange for the services that Britain has provided to you in recent years, I must ask you to do this for me. I am no average man, and I cannot be treated like one. *I* cannot end up in an underdeveloped country. God forbid! It doesn't bear thinking about! My very special circumstances must be considered. I implore you to organise my residency in the USA. I ask you to protect my life. *(Pause)* Perhaps I could even stay in the White House for a little while … until I've established myself once more? I've heard you're quite the host! ... What? ... You must have some influence … you are supposedly the most powerful man on the planet! *(Pause.)* Mr President, Britain has fully supported your foreign policy for the last decade, and she has also supported you through all the recent economic turbulence that we have encountered. This is in spite of the scorn and the resentment that we have experienced all on account of you, and for what? Continual embarrassment and scandal only! Mr President, if our loyalty in serving you holds any value whatsoever, I must ask you to use your influence to help me … Help me please …'

Some minutes later, the Prime Minister had slammed down the phone furiously, yanked it from its socket and thrown it out of the window. (*This caused the policeman on the door to look up … A sackable offence, I might add.*) Pure terror reigned in the Prime Minister's eyes. He had simultaneously lost control of the moment, of the country and of himself. He now felt weak. So weak, and so helpless. He felt the fear penetrate deep into his bones, he felt it manically pumping his blood around his body and he felt it lurking deep within his heart. It lurked there like death itself, as the shadow of insanity darkened his mind. What could he do to regain control? He needed money. That's it, he needed money! He must access his savings immediately. He would find someone to pay off in order to guarantee his safety. Yes, there would be someone ... there would definitely be someone! He managed to log on to his bank account quickly, despite his shaking fingers. The computer rapidly decelerated as it fought hard to connect to the chosen website. The bank's homepage flashed only one message before crashing:

'All services temporarily suspended.
Please try again later.'

The economic crisis had begun almost instantaneously. Despite his status as the most powerful man in Britain, the Prime Minister's account details were never made available to him again. His sound mind had also left him permanently. It disappeared with England. His destiny was no longer his own. (*Everyone always has the choice of how to react to different situations, and their reactions reveal the measure of their spirituality.*)

Regarding the last Prime Minister of Great Britain, or the 'iron man', legend has it that he sold his soul to the devil in exchange for a personality; for only a personality would help him to charm his way to the States!

When historians tried to track his movements many decades later, his last hours were recorded in a voodoo asylum. 'I have a sparkling personality,' he is said to have screamed at the workers repetitively, whilst being pinned down hard to a bed. His words went hand in hand with a blank, satanic glare, which the natives just did not trust. It was their job to get rid of the devil that had overtaken this individual, and they utilised all the possible traditional methods available to them to ensure that this happened. It was a severe case, but it is said that they eventually succeeded. Eventually, the Prime Minister was completely quiet. Completely cured and completely free.

4

Her angel's face,
As the great eye of heaven shined bright,
And made a sunshine in the shady place.
Edmund Spenser

In the two weeks that followed the secret meeting of the Heads of State in Washington DC, the plan – 'Operation Exodus' *(or O.E. as is later became known in the history books)* – was refined. Two weeks after the meeting, the press finally learnt of the crisis, and panic resonated through all continents like a crashing meteor. Even tribes in the Brazilian rainforest, who had never even caught a cold, caught wind of this situation. *The Cardiff Times* reported that the citizens of Wales were to be given a section of Australia *(for the Australians greatly appreciated their passion for rugby)* ... the red dragon was to dance freely in the Aussie outback. *The Glaswegian Herald* reported that the citizens of Scotland were to be given a large area of Russia to reside in, for, as *The Moscow Messenger* reported:

What could such expert whisky-makers do but help to propel the Vodka industry to even greater, never-before-seen profitability?

To a certain extent, Welsh and Scottish panic began slowly to subside. If truth be known, they actually began to celebrate

12

their God-ordained fate. (*Also celebrated was their new knowledge that they would no longer be shackled to the English! Some hoped that a hero-nation would come to the rescue of the English, but many hoped that the English would be left to drown alongside history's true memories.*)

What was the fate then of the citizens of England? One English paper reported that they were to be given free reign in Dubai. Another reported that the US was going to put aside a state for them to live in independently. Actually, neither story was accurate: in this critical situation, the burden of millions of English citizens was actually going to be shared out between all 'willing' countries, spanning six continents. The Great Council had had no time to run a fine toothcomb through O.E., for, at the time, Great Britain had already begun to sink uncontrollably. Momentum grew. All too suddenly, the priority was to get as many English residents as possible to their assigned countries, quickly and safely. The rest would be worked out within these countries, and according to each individual country's customs and laws, on arrival.

Residents began to fly to their assigned countries almost imme-diately, leaving nearly all of their worldly goods in the watery grave that would be the resting place of Britain's carcass. A woman from Wiltshire found herself in Germany. A family from Kent found itself in China. A man from Teeside found himself in Canada. Cornwall, Buckinghamshire, Merseyside – no more. Norfolk, Suffolk, Hertfordshire – no more. Now, English people were scattered all over the world – France, Spain, Portugal, Switzerland, Greece. The English were even squeezed into bulging Andorra. Poland, Ukraine, Bulgaria, Hungary, et cetera et cetera. Japan, India, Malaysia, Pakistan, et cetera et cetera. They even found some room in the skyscrapers of Hong Kong … even room in the most secret corners of Tibet. Zambia, South Africa, Kenya, Ghana, Nigeria,

Madagascar, et cetera et cetera. Brazil, Peru, Venezuela, Argentina. New Zealand, et cetera et cetera. Some of the lucky ones got Fiji. Some of the unlucky ones got Alaska (*hooded coats were, however, charitably supplied by the US Government*). Forced to follow in the footsteps of those who fled through parted waves, thousands frantically waved their strange goodbyes. Queue upon queue of aeroplanes cluttered up the runways of all British airports. The aeroplanes struggled to take off thanks to the sheer weight of a nation's burden.

England finally sank on a crisp, star-filled Christmas evening. In the early hours of the very same Christmas morning, the country was silent. The English nation missed their first wholly white Christmas for several years. They were not, however, saddened by this. All was quiet. So gentle … even pure snowflakes deafeningly hit the concrete streets. O.E. had, however, proved 'a success' according to global headlines. When England sank, the Queen went nowhere. She sat on her throne with her orb in her right hand, the crown jewels placed regally upon her head (*their impressive weight probably made the country sink that bit quicker!*). She was, at last, Spenser's fairy queen. The beefeaters stood stone-still at the Tower. Perfect loyalty. Snowflakes mystically floated onto their eyelashes. Wisdom really does come with winters! They did not blink once. All in a day's work for them … all in the line of duty. As the last beefeater steadfastly sank, the flapping of a raven's wings could be heard in the distance. Even the birds had taken the decision not to stay around.

Part Two

5

A banker had a dream one night, so vivid and so real, that it was much more than just a dream — for never had he experienced such faultless clarity, even when awake. He dreamt of a golden city, the splendour and spiritual perfection of which was beyond all human comprehension — only in a dream was it possible to understand and experience its full, translucent beauty … only on angels' wings. Humans lived together peacefully under Atlantis' rule. They had developed the faculties of Art and Science. These humans were so weirdly beautiful that they simply had to be a unique race … a legendary race. Mystic tribes.

The encapsulated moment was thousands of years past, but yet somehow, it also represented the future. Timeless. Too perfect …

Human weakness then set in. Mortal mistakes. Mortal greed. Fighting. Vandalism. Poseidon awoke from his deep slumber. He arose to the water's surface fiercely, and saw his perfect creation ruined. He was angry — his breath sent chilling shivers racing manically through the island. A single, golden trident can cause human catastrophe. The golden city began to suddenly sink under a gargantuan tidal wave. Deafening screams. Heartstopping hysteria. Eternal disappearance. The sea stole Atlantis' remaining treasures scornfully. The waves cruelly enveloped Atlantis' beautiful artwork punishingly. The irate ocean took Atlantis' new knowledge in one violent, laughing gush. The lost city sank, deep down, to the pitch black ocean bed. Deep down into the freezing cold, leaving only whispers of its perfection in the harsh, naive world above. Only echoes and whispers. A myth now. Reality no more … stirring …

… the people's remorseful tears still ride the waves senselessly …

... the purest culture on Earth was lost forever ...
The banker is stirring now...
Dream's metamorphosis.
A piercing voice commandingly states: 'London. You make money there, and then it will spit you out. Have you seen how tired and unfulfilled people look as you sit on the tube? Bitterness enveloping their eyelids. Mortal mistakes. Have you ever really noticed, banker? I said, have you ever really noticed, BANKER?!'

Buzz. Buzz. Buzz. Buzz.
He awoke.

The banker sat bolt upright. He was alone in his king-sized bed. Beads of sweat reigned victoriously on his forehead. The back of his neck was hot, clammy and wet.

Ordinarily, the banker would happily sleepwalk through life. He had always set his alarm for 06:30. He pressed 'snooze' once. (*Doze, doze, doze.*) He would spring out of bed on the second call, nine minutes later. He would watch the news channel, whilst eating a bowl of muesli (*completely naked regardless of the season, for, let it be noted that, during the winter months, the banker could afford the extravagant gas bills!*) He had muesli for breakfast, always with half a chopped banana in the bowl, and a scatter of pumpkin seeds – (*these ingredients helped his immune system to stay strong, so that he would never have to miss a day of his beloved work*). He would clean his teeth, always with the same brand of toothpaste. He would rinse his mouth out, always with the same brand of mouthwash. He would shower, always using the same brand of shower gel. His towels were all the same royal blue colour, embroidered with his initial – 'W' – (*which provided the banker with a feeling of incredible self-worth*). He

18

would return to the kitchen and enjoy a cup of good old English breakfast tea with one sugar, before he set off to work from his Surrey Quays one-bedroomed, river-view flat. (*He was so proud of his one-bedroomed, river-view flat, which had dramatically risen in value during the last decade ... 'Aren't I clever?' the banker would often think to himself.*) He would leave his one-bedroomed, river view flat at 07:30, in order to get the 07:42 tube from Canada Water into the city. In this twelve-minute window, he would make the daily purchase of his oversized newspaper.

Even though he could have left later, the banker would get the 07:42 train to ensure he had a seat for his journey. This enabled him to study the valid sections of his newspaper. His special interest was in the financial section, for the banker fancied himself as a bit of an investor. Shrewd investment, he thought, would ensure that he made his first million by the time he reached 50! It was true that he had been fairly successful on a small scale, but he was yet to reap the rewards – he had, four years ago, splashed out £10,000 to participate in a course, entitled 'Beating the Stock Market and Making it Your Own'.

Immersed in this morass of numbers, the banker never looked at any of the other passengers. He failed to notice the lifeless look in so many pairs of eyes. A bitter expression in so many others. Suspicion always runs riot. He unconsciously blocked out the tangible air of depression lingering throughout the whole tube train.

The banker would get into London Bridge at approximately 07:46. He would walk to the office and arrive there at about 08:01. He would make his way up to the tenth floor of the bank's headquarters via the lift. When he reached the office and, depending on how risqué he was feeling, he might stop to hold a brief, monotone discussion with a colleague (*never more than one mind*) for 30 to 40 seconds.

By 08:15, he would have logged onto his computer. He was proud of the fact that he gave his company an extra 45 minutes of his time on a daily basis − *(for he was a team player, and he understood how he could personally contribute to maximising the efficiency and profitability for the bank in which he worked)*. This was the bank he lived and breathed for. Part of the banker's job was to maintain databases, which held thousands upon thousands of customer details. He had even once had the privilege of handling the Prime Minister's bank details! Even the banker couldn't resist having an extra long glance at those − *(he experienced a sense of overwhelming guilt afterwards though, and had a bath as soon as he got home in order to cleanse himself of the sinful feeling which had satanically taken over him)*. Despite this one-off dance with the devil, the banker took his job extremely seriously. He was, in his own rather archaic words, 'a loyal devil!' No mention of the bank would ever pass from his lips, for he was paranoid … paranoid about the true identity of those characters with whom he chose to engage in his dull conversations.

Every day, at 13:00, he would go to lunch with a fellow banker. He trusted this particular man, and, in his head, classified him as a friend! There they would talk together about money, property and new electrical devices in perfectly synchronised and perfectly dull, monotone voices.

They would both begin work again by 13:55.

Sometimes the banker would have a meeting in the afternoon. Apart from that, he would conscientiously continue the work he had begun in the morning.

The banker would leave work at 17:35, getting the 17:51 tube back home. He would arrive back at Canada Water by approximately 18:08 and would be opening the front door by about 18:20. He would cook his dinner and have a German beer *(yes, a beer!)* He would joyously log onto his laptop by 19:40, where

20

he would enter the world of virtual friends for a while. Sometimes he would even be brave enough to flirt with a faceless, lonely female. On such occasions, he would 'relieve himself', whilst simultaneously checking his e-mails – trying to glean more global financial information as he climaxed. He would go to bed at 22.30. If for any reason he was still pottering around at 22:31, he would break out into a panicked, cold sweat.

The banker was now 35, and had been following this same obsessive routine for eleven years. This was the banker's life. It's what made him feel happy. It's what made him tick. It was not, however, the dictates of his soul, as he had previously thought … for, he was sleepwalking … and he always had been sleepwalking. Until *that* morning.

When O.E. was made public on 6 October 2013, with the PM's national broadcast, the banker awoke suddenly from a nightmare. His surreal nightmare had been about sinking Atlantis. He awoke to a strange new world. His own dark reality:

Blankness…
Bombardment…

My money.
    My flat.
        My job.
            The tube.
                My newspapers.
                    My muesli.
                        My bonuses.
MY MONEY!

The banker left his bowl of muesli that day, and he didn't shower. He sat, in a trance, on his brown leather sofa for a while. The lines of the speech were ringing over and over again in his ears. His one small comfort at that moment was that his brown leather sofa felt so cold ... so soothing. He rubbed his plump, naked arm against the material for several minutes. (*How he loved that brown leather sofa!*) He put his forehead against it for a few moments. 'I've neither showered nor cleaned my teeth this morning. Good Lord!' the banker thought to himself, shocked.

It was his instinct to get to work though, and, get to work he did!

... Trance-like.

He arrived at work 'late' that day, having missed the early train. As a result of this, he did not give the bank an extra 45 minutes of his time. He naively logged onto his computer at 09:00. Somehow, his dedication was still innate within him. However, he logged onto a global crisis. By 09:01, customers were withdrawing their savings, whilst they still could. The world stock market was collapsing crazily and scarily fast. Soon after this, the banker's PC crashed like a broken rollercoaster (*and they had said that it could continue to run during any disaster. Ha!*) He was, for the first time, a useless entity in the banking world. Null and void. His status was being forcefully ripped from him, and his perfect, routine life was being cruelly snatched away. He was helpless.

... *But* he was beginning to wake up now at least.

There was nothing the banker could do at work that day, and so, somehow, for the first time, he began to talk to his colleagues about what this dark world and cruel future meant for them all. *Really talk* I mean. Hands were held, tears shed and the suited men embraced one another: the pinstripes embraced the

22

checkered, the black suits embraced the grey suits and the bright ties embraced the dull ties. The men even embraced their female colleague, as an equal, for the first time. Wails filled the room as all manner of numbers, figures, decimal points and currencies plummeted and cascaded on the foreboding screens before them. The men did not go home that night. They stared, shiny-eyed at these figures all night long in fact. They were devastated, and the world was furious. Furious with sinking Britain. Stubble even began to appear on a few of the bank workers' faces. They caught a whiff of each other's body odours, but it mattered not now, for they suddenly knew each other intimately. Not sleeping, but holding hands, the men – and the woman – knew that they possessed nothing now ... except this moment together. (*And how they cherished each other's company, for they knew that they had lost everything – everything that they had ever worked for.*) Yesterday, normality reigned. Normality was a conning farce though. They had been sleepwalking, and they were now all waking up. Fast. And there they remained in the office's comforting embrace all day long. For a time, they managed to block from their minds the reality that they would have to make their way back to their homes very, very soon.

By the end of the day, they had been asked to leave the premises 'within the next two hours' by an unknown man.

'Please, don't make us go!' one man cried out in agonising pain.

'We must stay here until everything returns to normal – things will be back to normal soon, won't they?!' shrieked another. He looked up towards the heavens and raised his arms in the air pleadingly. (*Ironically, he had always considered himself an atheist, until this particular moment in time.*)

'I need to sleep,' whispered the banker. He was exhausted. Drained.

With the exception of the banker, all of the hypnotised men – and the woman – immediately and instinctively parted company with a distant handshake. They could not say goodbye to one another. The words refused to pour out of their lips, but, nevertheless, they did leave the building.

They never saw each other again.

The banker, however, fell asleep curled up on the office carpet. There he remained until he was kicked out of what had been his life, one hour and fifty minutes later. Soon after this, the office building was nothing more than an architectural skeleton. Totally deserted. A symbol of a nation's former might and domination. So quickly snatched away.

The banker found himself at the tube station. He couldn't remember the walk there. It must have been raining, for he was soaking wet. He waited two hours for the tube that evening. It did not matter though, for he had completely lost all concept of time in that particular moment. Time did not exist for him any more.

When he did finally find himself standing, squashed, in the moving tube, he began to look at all the passengers one by one. He studied their faces really closely. Many faces were tear-stained, and several ghostly faces were pearl-drop white. The banker carefully studied an elderly man, whose face was recovering from a fierce invasion of nasty bruises – all shades of purple, brown, yellow and blue mockingly cascaded over his face. Something wholly evil had happened to this gentleman and, in the depths of his eyes, a nothingness had overpowered him and usurped his soul. The banker sensed that the bruises themselves bowed down to Lucifer. This very real figure had a deep and lasting affect on the banker, and, even in light of the dramatic circumstances of the day, his heart raced with shock. His senses were heightened.

On this new level of alert, the banker randomly noticed an attractive young lady seated near him, who was around 20 years of age. As she raised her hands to embrace her face, a book dropped out of her lap to the ground. Her hands moved over her pale face eerily, and, as she shook her head from side to side, her blonde curls danced about her shoulders. Deeply feeling her pain, something new ignited inside the banker. He speechlessly and empathetically bonded with her – although they, too, never spoke. When the tube paused, he picked up her book – *The Complete Works of Shakespeare* – and placed it on the young lady's lap, unnoticed by her. Years later, the banker could remember nothing of this panic period. He did, however, remember the surprising and unexplained feelings of intimacy that he had felt towards that nameless young lady. That young lady whom he never even spoke to.

The banker slept in a feverish state for six days and six nights. On the seventh day, the flat buzzer brought him back to his living nightmare with a thud.
He stirred.
Buzzer.
Waking.
Angry buzzer.
Waking-up.
What a furious buzzer!
The banker fell out of bed, and weakly crawled to his receiver.
'Hello, who is it?'
'I have a special delivery for you'
'Oh … OK … Come up please.' (*In spite of the situation in which the banker now found himself, he never disregarded his normal, courteous tone.*)
Buzzzzzzz.

Angry, tired feet were climbing the steps quickly.

'(*Tut*) ... Please sign here ... (*Tut*).'

Furious, tired feet were now descending down the steps even more quickly (*and tuts could be heard all the way down*).

Still neither in a restful nor a wakeful state, the banker walked to the mirror. Bearded and thin, he did not recognise himself. His pulse seemed to stop for a second, and he became breathless. He ran to the kitchen and drank four pints of water, hardly managing to breathe in his struggle to swallow. He vomited liquid, but did not wipe his beard clean. He felt utterly petrified. Gasping for air, he groped his way to his brown leather sofa – he had to lean against the wall and use his arms to support himself along the way. He sat there like a statue for an hour, two hours ... maybe even three hours ... he knew not how long he sat there. It did not matter though – he had nowhere to go. He looked closely at the envelope that he had been given. He peeled it open carefully and with reluctance.

One A5 piece of paper revealed to the banker the country to which he would soon be relocated. William J. Smith was wide awake now.

6

STUDENT MONEYLENDERS COMPANY
ANNUAL STATEMENT

Balance Brought Forward   24,231.50

20/09/2013
Interest
223.50

New Balance   24,455.00

(*I'm hungover.*)

The student had felt blasé, until she glanced at her annual statement.

(*Feeling sick.*)

Everyone else was borrowing, so why should she waste her time worrying about it?

(*My head's pounding.*)

Her forehead screwed up tight as she tried to remember the events of the preceding night. The cocktail bar (*pricy, but too drunk to care*), the vodka bar (*student prices – took advantage of that ... feeling really sick now*). Yes, she'd sampled a wide range of disgustingly flavoured vodkas, but she felt true regret now. She'd kissed a random student – a law undergraduate as she recalled.

(*Real remorse.*)

Today she would turn over a new leaf though. Today she had three things to worry about – (*in reality, this was quite a lot compared with a typical day*):

1. English Tutorial – 11 am
2. English Lecture – 3 pm
3. Going out.

The student was, however, already a failure: she glanced at her watch, and it was 10:45. The Professor would be seriously annoyed with her now. (*He was so easily offended by people that did not share his passion for Shakespeare!*) She'd make an effort to get to her 3 o'clock lecture at least. She lay down on her bed. (*Groan.*) She covered her face with her hands, longing to feel normal once again. (*Actually, what was 'normal' for her now?*) ... Ah well, everyone else was doing it, she reassured herself ...

The student awoke some hours later to a sustained buzzing sound. The September sun shone peculiarly through her curtains. (*Indian summer?*) She found the brightness both disturbing and irritating. 'I'm sure the sun never used to shine so brightly in September,' the student thought, 'No wonder there are so many confused wasps around!' After ten minutes of trying to ignore the ferocious buzzing, the student finally forced herself to open the window.

In the moment before the wasp stung her, the student noticed a flash of red and black stripes – there was no yellow to be seen.

Distorted nature.

Sickly Mother Earth.

The sting was wholly unexpected, and the student, terrified, gasped out with sheer pain. She had been stung before, but it

28

hadn't felt like this. The pain enveloped her whole body. She dropped to the ground and froze. She shivered and she perspired. Her eyes eerily beamed with an enigmatic glaze. The student tried to scream out, but no sound left her mouth.
SILENCE.

She tried to crawl to the door, but horrified, she realized she was completely paralysed. The air that she inhaled felt thick with devilish deceit. She eventually fell into an agonisingly uncomfortable sleep on the carpet.

Although the pain of the wasp sting faded in time, it never left the student. It's dull, disgusting sensation remained with her for the rest of her life. Needless to say, she did not make it to her 3 o'clock lecture that day.

The student made no mention to anybody of the festering pain that spread through her body over the next couple of weeks. Whenever she attempted to, her mouth would seize up, and the pain would return, momentarily paralysing her. So, she gave up after a while. She became withdrawn in conversations with her friends; she sounded ghostly in telephone conversations to her family.

Her mother implored her father to visit their daughter …

'Please, let's go see her. Something's happened to her. We need to try and find out what's happened to her.'

He stood firm.

'Yes, it's natural that you feel this way, dearest. Look … I know it's difficult, but she is developing into a young lady, and we must learn to let go of her.'

Her friends tried to cheer her up patiently …

'Come out tonight – it will do you good.'

The student merely shook her head vacantly, and wandered away from them. She had to escape them.

(Even the Professor agreed a two-week extension on her essay without debate, for he sensed the magnitude of her inner tsunami.)

One week and six days of the extension had now passed. The student sat, locked in her room, her laptop on, face to face with the wordless document. She felt as empty and blank as the paper. She typed slowly and painfully, not noticing how deadly-pale her hands looked:

'Shylock. Victim or Villain?'

She did not add anything further. She couldn't. She merely picked up her bag and walked out of her room like a zombie. She never returned. Within the hour, she was sitting on a train to London. She didn't know why.

Funny. In her two and a half years at university studying English Literature, the student had not read a single book from cover to cover. It was away from university, in an all-night café, that she first connected with Shakespeare. The edition of the book she now carried had always been precious to her – for, on learning of her precious granddaughter's university place, her grandmother had proudly passed down her very own copy of *The Complete Works of Shakespeare* shortly before her death. That night in London the words within the book entranced the student's heart.

Shylock was unlikeable, that was true, and his demand was gruesome. But then, was this born out of the scorn that he constantly experienced from those surrounding him? He was different from everybody else, and people immediately and automatically felt a strong contempt for him. That was unfair – he did not have a choice in living and trading amongst people who were 'different' to him. How cruel to be forced into a world where you are unwelcome … looked upon as a villain, but really a victim. A baby that was loved once. Despised now. And what was debt anyway? (*Her mind flashed back to her recently received student loan statement.*) Was it the merchant's attempt to gain some kind of status, some superiority, some feeling of self-worth? (*If she couldn't repay her debt, would the Loans Company demand a pound of her flesh?*) No. Debt is a means of control. It is the false illusion that you are working towards a better future. It is the foundation on which a false country is run. Greedy people making money on debt. Greedier people profiting from debt's debt. No real capital. No real substance. Sheer stupidity …. good job. House. Car. Holidays. Twice a year. You get these things, but you don't *really* get them. False illusions.

Which was the greater burden: Antonio's debt or Shylock's background? Victorious, popular Antonio. Ever-hated Shylock.

The student stayed in the café all night. Alone. Her only company was her *Complete Works*, her hardback notebook and her thoughts. Tiredness never set in. She began to feel real for the first time. (*A first step into adulthood, maybe?*) There she remained, in a trance-like state, until 6 am, when a tragic newsflash was broadcast to the nation and to the rest of the world …

Suddenly wide awake, the student spent a few desperate hours trying to get through to her family by phone. But this was impossible. All the while, cars were honking manically outside and people were crying hysterically. She watched loved ones embracing one another. She watched strangers embracing one another. She saw people sprinting outside. She saw people lying stone-still in the street. She eventually reached her father, who spoke slowly. Very slowly. He was trying to be strong, but his voice shook in a way that she had never heard before. It was only then that she realised that this was a real crisis. (*Strong fathers were now weak and vulnerable.*) Yet, somehow this man continued to pull his sentences together ... somehow. He asked his little girl to get home as soon as she could – just get to a train station, and wait for a train, no matter how long it took. Force yourself onto a train, no matter who gets in your way.

The student had nearly run out of money, and so she quickly went to a cash point. The screen was blank, though. Completely dead. Only then did she notice the street-long queue, which led into the doors of the bank. She would have to join the queue, for, without money, she had no chance of getting home. Families waited in the queue, the elderly waited in the queue, teenagers waited in the queue. There was even a lottery winner crying out in the queue, desperate to hold on to his brand-new dream life – (*it was running away from him though, and it was laughing deceptively as it ran. It sprinted so quickly...*)

The student waited in the queue all day, but to no avail. There was no money to be had. Several of the bank workers had been assaulted, and sat lifelessly at their desks with panda-black eyes, shutters down. The police had arrived to try to pacify this new wave of panicked, frenzied hatred. The student tried to phone home, but the phone line was now completely dead. No chance! The silence that had resonated from the receiver still hurt her ears several minutes later. She walked towards a small park, where she sat on a bench. In her weakness she allowed herself to cry now. She allowed herself this one indulgence. She cried because of what had happened at the bank. She cried for her own life, and for the lives of her family and friends. They were all about to be catapulted into a dark, strange place ... a dark, strange new world. Everyone.

A kindly woman sat next to her. She did not speak at first.

Her aura, however, immediately consoled the young student. It really did. Sometime later, the almost saintly lady spoke gently in a strong Liverpudlian accent.

'Where will you go now, love? Do you have a family to see?'

'I can't get home. I haven't got the money for the train.'

The woman gave the student £50 without hesitation – she was prophetically adamant that money would have no value very, very soon. The fifty-pound note would be of no use to her or to anyone else! *(Egoless, guardian angels always shimmer brightly in the midst of a crisis.)* Relieved and grateful, the student briskly walked to the nearest tube station, all the while protectively clutching her grandmother's book, which now had the crisp fifty-pound note pressed firmly inside its inner cover. She waited for some time at the ticket machines.

Initially, as the carriage pulled away, the student had to stand. However, she soon managed to get a seat. She felt very weak and dehydrated at this point. A sudden surge of emotion enslaved her. She raised her hands to embrace her face, and they moved over her pale face eerily. Her face felt clammy. As she shook her head from side to side, she heard her book drop to the floor. She was too weak to pick it up.

She came to her senses some minutes later. When she finally freed her face from her hands, the first thing she noticed was her precious book sitting in her lap. *(How did that get there?)* This was a surreal sign of hope for her. And she felt real once again. Just for a moment, she felt safe and protected. Only for a split second mind you ... optimism then violently got sucked into the ensuing darkness.

7

The disaster, when it happened, was unexpectedly severe. Soon after the fall of the rocks (which was relatively small) the tremendous power of the insurgent water swept away a huge portion of the retaining rock face. All of the Atlantians, who were enjoying leisure activities and meditation in the beautiful areas below the middle slopes of the valley, were lost to the raging floodwater. The extent of the disaster was greater than had been expected, for the feed of the water to the inland lake had been underesti-mated. When the flooding finally settled, a group of islands remained of those parts of Atlantis that were above sea level. Jeham was lost in the tragedy, along with many of the elderly Atlantians, who had spent most of their time in the depths of the valleys.

George W. Gee

The Colonel had served his country as a young man during World War II. He had been well respected by all the men he had ever encountered during this period. (*Well remembered by only a small minority now … forgotten by too many.*) During the Second World War, he had been very willing to serve England, for he did not want his children and grandchildren growing up in a German-speaking country. (*He'd be damned if they grew up in a German-speaking country!*)

During the war, no one could have ever imagined the atroc-ities that had taken place throughout Europe. How could they have done? It was only in the post-war years that the full scale and the terrifying truth – regarding the Jewish genocide – was made public. More than six million killed. This race of people had never been accepted into the world. Judged daily, wherever their homes were, and however they lived. (*But, has the world really learnt from past mistakes and incomprehensible tragedy? To what extent has this lesson really been absorbed?*)

In the post-war decades, the Colonel remained steadfastly proud that he had 'done his bit' for the nation, and he was also proud that he had made a small contribution to bringing about an end to the 'goddamned Nazi regime'. On special occasions, he would wear his medals, which encapsulated both his contribution and his pride. Strangers would beam at him with gratitude. All the sacrifice and effort had been well worth it, he would think to himself on days such as this.

No one spoke to him any more. All people saw now was an elderly pest-like man, draining their taxes. The Colonel did not feel like a man any more. He would never admit that to anybody, though. At 88 years old, he possessed only feelings of weakness and worthlessness, and these weighed heavily on his heart. His daughter phoned him once a week, but, as far as he could see, this was purely to nag him: it was evidently her life's mission to get him to move into a care home. He was a burden to her ... only ever a burden. The Colonel's daughter had her own family and job to worry about, and, although she never said it, the Colonel knew that he was a splash of discomfort that tainted her otherwise very 'perfect' life. He knew the extent to which his very existence irritated her.

'Why doesn't the stubborn old fool move into a home? He's always struggling to pay his bills and his small flat is ice-cold during winter!'

(*Nag. Nag. Nag.*)

His thoughts would wander ... I am ice-cold with loneliness too, for I miss my beautiful wife.

The Colonel was not looking forward to the impending winter. He was, indeed, dreading it …

Two weeks before the Prime Minister's announcement, the Colonel had been visiting an old friend, whom he had not seen for two years. They shared a lovely day together, exchanging memories in a way that only comrades can. The Colonel felt like a real man again for one afternoon. Time had run away from them, and, before they knew it, it was dark and it was getting very late. The Colonel ordered a taxi to the tube station (*because he could not afford a damned taxi for the whole journey home*). He felt unnerved on the deserted platform. Silence both boomed and echoed deafeningly. He covered his ears in pain. A rat danced through the shadowy train lines with no fear, smirking up patronisingly at the elderly figure.

Finally on board the tube, the Colonel shared a carriage with two young teenagers. He began to relax. (*He stupidly began to relax.*) He noticed that both youngsters were wearing Spurs shirts. He noticed this, for he too had always supported Tottenham Hotspur FC. Looking further down the carriage, he noticed a suited man, whose face was hidden behind an oversized newspaper. The Colonel's attention returned to the boys, and he smiled affectionately at them for their choice in loyalty. (*At least something was being passed passionately from generation to generation!*) But then he began to look deeper at their faces … deeper into their angry, young faces. Why were these youngsters so bitter? They hadn't been forced to serve their country. They had food. Where had yesterday's warmth disintegrated to? It was so sad. How is it that laughing babies metamorphose into such unfulfilled, empty human beings so quickly? No hope for the future! 'There is almost a fennel look to those eyes,' continued the Colonel in his own head, 'Why did I fight? Why did I lose so many friends for those wild, bitter eyes?'

'What are you fucking looking at, old man?!'

Such hate. Such bitterness. The tone of the teenager brought the Colonel bumpily back to earth. He had not realised he'd been staring at the elder youth quite so intently.

'You deaf!?'

He was shouting. Screaming almost. The younger Spurs supporter laughed savagely and lifelessly. The hate scraped the Colonel's ears and left a permanent dent on his, already, heavily burdened soul. He felt so vulnerable and so scared. (*He hated that once foreign feeling so much! Youth was his comrade no longer, but decades were now his burden.*) He tried to open his mouth, but he couldn't speak. The younger Spurs supporter got his phone out, and pointed it at the Colonel. This confused the elderly man, for he did not understand what was going on. He jumped hard, for he thought he was being shot at. He protected his head and his body with his arms. This caused the boys to descend to new levels of devilishly scarlet, penetrating laughter. The elder youth, who had spoken to the Colonel a few moments earlier, walked over to him and punched him once in the face. The soldier felt petrified. He could do nothing. No man's land. He covered his face. He then felt a hard, animal-like thump on the back of his head.

Heartless.

Inhumane.

Ice-cold.

New extremes of heaviness.

Blackness.

SILENCE.

The Colonel came round in hospital a few hours later. He had been discovered by a woman, who had got on the tube a couple of stops after the attack. She was so concerned about him, that she visited him in hospital a few times in the days following the attack. Trapped in his own terrible emptiness, the Colonel experienced a tiny, tiny glimmer of light for the last time, due to this woman's selfless actions. The Colonel's daughter had also gone out of her way to visit him twice as well. To his surprise, she held him tight for several minutes, when she first saw him in the hospital bed. The darkness soon monstrously – and inevitably – swallowed up the light, though.

During the next few days, the Colonel spoke to the police about what had happened. They had looked concerned at the time, he had thought, but nothing much was done about it. They informed the Colonel that they had tried to trace the suited man, who had been reading the oversized newspaper, but to no avail. And so, the Colonel's claim was sent off to the Criminal Injuries Department. He would hear back in the next few months, they assured him. (*So, how is it that the authorities, who act like Big Brother, can wrongly give every second person a parking ticket and have evidence 'on film', yet they can't catch the criminals who mercilessly assault an elderly, patriotic man? A nation's distorted, disfigured priorities stupidly parade in front of us, bellowing with laughter.*)

The Colonel was soon discharged. He could not afford the taxi home, so he got the tube. *Déjà vu.* His heart raced horribly for the whole journey. Any slight movement made him jump and gasp out loud. Inside his flat, he treble-locked the door from the inside.

Although his face slowly began to heal in the days that followed, his heart never did. He was dead inside now. He stayed in his flat, and his daughter brought him his meals. She never stayed long though. The intimacy had now disappeared, and she could no longer look him in the eye. It was as if she was ashamed of him …

When the Prime Minister made his announcement, the

Colonel felt nothing. It made no difference to him, for he was filled up with such empty heaviness anyway. He would experience fear no more. It no longer mattered to him that he had fought long and hard to save this country. Not in the least.

About a week later, a letter arrived informing him that his designated country was Germany. His last ever trip out of his flat was to the O.E. office to tell them that he refused to go to that damned country, thank you very much. He'd rather die than end up living in Germany! They did not care though. They did not listen to this ranting, mad, old man. (*They merely mocked him during their cigarette break outside – to them, he was just a mild glimmer of amusement in these dark, scary times.*) In an entirely patronising manner, they gave him his instructions for packing and travel, robotically disregarding and disrespecting his reasons for refusal. On the journey home, the Colonel's feeling of foreboding emptiness expanded still further. He noticed a shocked, suited gentleman staring hard at his still-bruised face, but the Colonel felt nothing. He cared no longer. 'Let him stare,' he thought lifelessly. 'Let him see what kind of a country this is. I am England! You can wake me up when this has all ended … when this has all gone!'

The Colonel passed away in his sleep that night. He had refused to go to Germany, and so, it seemed that there was no other choice for him. When the Colonel's daughter found his body two days later, he was holding his most prized medal in his hand. The other medals she later found in his wicker bin. She held his freezing-cold hand up to her face and cried. She did this despite the already intoxicating smell that danced around the icy flat – a putrid concoction of cruelty, failure, disregard and neglect.

On the same night that the Colonel died, images of an old

man being attacked on a London tube were viewed on the internet by 122 faceless people around the world. They had all searched for 'fights'. (*Hardly a fight, but entertaining enough though. Many of them laughed at what they saw.*)

This is a fast sinking world – a world that is indeed sinking as fast as lost Atlantis did. Yet, with pride wholly in tact, an Atlantian elder once disappeared fast into the eternal abyss. Undignified, an English elder was left to drown under a decade's weight of disrespecting darkness. Worlds apart.

8

*A nation which has forgotten its past
can have no future.*
Sir Winston Churchill

The only time that the two young Spurs supporters felt truly
alive was when they watched their team playing football. They
enjoyed experimenting with different types of drugs, when they
could afford it. They enjoyed an extra-hot curry, when they
could afford it. Most days, they got a buzz when they played
each other on their games consoles or surfed the net together.
However, they only truly and purely came to life when watching
a game of football. They loved the feeling of oneness they
experienced with every other supporter. It gave their life some
meaning – some meaning where there otherwise was none.
They both lived for that feeling of euphoria when a goal was
scored. They both lived for the mass chanting of the club songs
echoing around the stadium. They lived for Premiership points.
They inhaled European points. They hung on the every word
of their manager, and they would have kissed the boots of
every player if they'd been given half the chance!

Yet, football only came around once a week – twice a week,
if they were lucky. For the other 165 hours of the week, the
young Spurs supporters were both bored and frustrated. And
they sucked each other deeper into this void, like over-powerful

magnets. They had left school the previous year, having learnt virtually nothing. (*The teachers had fought a losing battle with 'that class of no-hopers' both physically and mentally.*) The elder Tottenham supporter had always found it hard at school, for he was behind his peers anyway. He had come to England as an asylum seeker seven years earlier, having no prior knowledge of the English language. At first, he had worked hard to catch up, but, under-achieving, he fell into the ways of the other children after a while. He had, therefore, never achieved anywhere near the required level in any of the core subjects. He masked this domi-nating sense of failure with the one-dimensional persona that he had created for himself … he disguised his fast-dying dreams with rudeness and hatefulness.

When they both left school, neither boy had the qualifica-tions to get any kind of a decent job. The jobs they had both managed to get were so dull, that they would, by now completely demotivated, lose their tempers very quickly. (*They both lost their tempers very quickly indeed!*) It was, consequently, no surprise to anyone, including themselves, that they had both been sacked on a number of occasions already. They had lost all will and ambition to gain a job now, and generally spent their dole cheques on pot, lager and food, whilst still relying fully on their ignorant, spaced-out mums.

Shortly after leaving school, the younger Spurs supporter managed to impregnate a 15-year-old girl. The boy had wanted to try to be a good dad to the baby at first − (*something he, himself, had never experienced*). However, his mother had gone ballistic. He thought about it carefully for a couple of minutes, and decided that he did not want to leave home − he'd be crazy to! He did not have to pay rent there and his meals were always cooked for him − he, therefore, chose to ignore the fact that he was going to become a father. This did not bother the girl too much, for a dad in the picture would have severely reduced her chances of laying her hands on a council flat. (*In fact, before she had even been given a council flat, she was already trying to become impregnated by another randomly stoned teenager, in order to get an even bigger property.*) The younger Spurs supporter never met his child.

Both youths had recently begun to get even more bored than usual.

Bored.

Bored.

Bored.

Bored.

Bored.

Neither youngster could be sure when or how it happened, but they gradually began to gain some warped kind of a pleasure from belittling strangers … hurting strangers too. (*This is the product of children born in a violent age, born into one mould only. Maybe Milton was right after all: it is better to reign in hell than to serve in heaven.*)

It had started off on a small scale at first for the two youths – pushing a smaller kid into a wall, for example – nothing too hardcore. Now, it had reached a new, disgusting level, culminating in a vicious attack on an old man, which they had also filmed using a mobile phone. Both felt guilty after this attack. Neither boy, however, would admit this to one another. They were not allowed to feel such emotions in each other's company … it was forbidden! Once the footage was online, they would artificially brag to their friends, pretending to marvel at the growing number of hits on their footage – it had now reached 2,743 viewings in only a couple of weeks. This marvel was fake though – deep down, both Spurs supporters felt awful. Deep, deep down, they were both plagued by devilish, invisible remorse.

When O.E. was underway, both boys were, in fact, relieved to be leaving the dark, corrupting influence of the other. All they saw was all they knew, and they both desired a new, more positive experience. The family of the younger English-born Spurs supporter was allocated India as their destination. However – like all asylum seekers – the elder Tottenham supporter's family had been designated back to their home country. Fear grew rapidly amongst the British asylum seeker population, for they were being forced back to face whatever it was that they had initially run away from. They knew how they would be punished when they returned. They didn't have a choice though. The elder boy's family members could feel death's putrid breath on their faces once more. Both families had to leave in a rush – one family had five days before their flight, the other family had just four. Both families followed the official instructions, which specified each person must take one small case only. Both youths packed their football shirts first. (*The elder supporter left behind his mobile phone, for it had begun to make him feel sick even to touch it.*) The boys wished each other luck, but they did not shake hands with one another. They had no intention of attempting to stay in contact. As a consequence, the younger supporter never found out that his once best friend had been executed within two months of leaving England. (*Poetic justice some might say?*)

The younger supporter could, himself, never bury the memories of the months that had led up to the mass evacuation of England. He could never forget them, even though he had been given the opportunity of travelling thousands of miles across the globe to try to escape their almighty grip. Even though he had been given the opportunity to try and make a fresh start for himself, these stormy memories continued to forcefully penetrate the depths of his conscious and subconscious day in and day out.

Years later, a stranger asked the younger Spurs supporter:
  'What was it like in England?'
  'England was a dark place. It sucked you into the darkness.'
  On another occasion, a young, inquisitive child asked the now elderly man:
  'What does it feel like to be old?'
  The younger supporter thought about the question carefully ... thought about how it really felt. He did not feel like a man anymore. At 88 years old, the younger Spurs supporter possessed only feelings of ice-cold weakness and worthlessness. He cried in front of the child, who was standing before him, and who was staring intently and deeply into his guilty eyes. The elderly man was convinced that the child saw everything. He began to shed tears of remorse for the act that he had carried out more than seven decades earlier. The face of the elderly man on the tube haunted his mind vividly, and, in that face, he now saw only himself.

9

What feeds me destroys me.
Christopher Marlowe

The Colonel's daughter loved her life. She loved her house, which her and her husband had purchased twelve years earlier. It had risen by over £200,000 in value since then. Can you believe it? (*'Aren't we clever?', the married couple would often exclaim to each other.*) This impressive sum would have actually risen even more since their last valuation, as they had shrewdly built a conservatory recently! On sunny days, the married couple would sit in their newly built conservatory, which overlooked their large, symmetrical garden. They would think to themselves, 'aren't we clever?' They would say to one another, 'aren't we clever?' Pure, untainted happiness. They were not only keeping up with the Jones, but ignorantly overtaking them. (*Ha, ha, HA!*)

Life had been quieter since their two sons had both left for university. Their elder son was a law undergraduate; the younger had opted for a mathematics degree. Both parents were so very proud of them both. Sitting in their conservatory, they would talk about their clever sons. So sensible – what futures both of them had ahead of them! Every few weeks, the sons would return home for the weekend. (*The boys would co-ordinate the same*

46

weekend to please their mother – what a close-knit family they were!) The Colonel's daughter would be in her element cooking a Sunday roast on such weekends – how her boys loved their darling mother's Sunday roast!

In the evenings, the married couple would sit on their fashionably cream sofa, watching their plasma TV – what a TV it was! Cinema-like in proportions, hundreds of channels, screen as flat as a pancake. They would happily flick between the channels, thinking how hard they'd both worked for their beautiful plasma TV. How they both deserved that gorgeous telly!

Bla, bla, bla, bla, bla!

'Are you okay, dear?' the husband would check.

'I'm fine, darling,' the Colonel's daughter would beam back. In her husband's eyes, she was a radiant being. (*In her husband's eyes only!*) Weren't they the most perfectly happy, clever, deserving couple you ever did see? The Colonel's daughter would often smile to herself, as her eyes left the screen and wandered up to their silver-framed wedding photo, which was 25 years old this year. It sat perfectly on their perfect TV. They would often talk about their dream home in Italy, which they hoped to buy next year. Their eyes would widen with excitement, their fingers would wriggle quickly with contagious greed at the thought of their very own second, retirement home. (*Their fingers had to move quickly, as they would now need to wipe away the gluttonous foam that had begun to form on each side of their mouths.*) Imagine ... a second home. How very clever they were!

Every morning, the married couple would enjoy a mug of real, percolated coffee together. 'None of this instant lark,' the husband would exclaim authoritatively. He always kissed his wife on her left cheek just before he left for work. He would get into his flash black Jag. (*You know what they say about men with Jags!*) He did not care that the car guzzled petrol, he deserved to drive his 'beauty'. He would reverse her expertly out of the drive. Delighted with this impressive manoeuvring exhibition, the Colonel's daughter would wave out of the window and clap in sheer delight, jumping up and down in orgasmic excitement. For a few minutes after this, she would feel a little sad that she would not see her husband until the evening ... apart from that though, she was perfectly happy.

Half an hour later, the Colonel's daughter herself would be reversing her car out of the garage ready to go to work. She did not reverse as smoothly, or as confidently, as her husband had done (*she would not have wanted to*) – nevertheless, she exited out of the garage satisfactorily enough. On her drive to work, the Colonel's daughter would often sing along to the radio and laugh at the quick wit of the posh presenters.

Soon enough, a feeling of darkness would always begin to swamp her though ...

She must ring her father tonight, she must travel into London to visit him this weekend.

They had never been close – he had always been so distant, so hard throughout her childhood. Well, that was when he had actually been there that is! They had drifted even further apart following her mother's death. His stubborn, selfish streak meant that she constantly had to worry about him and to take responsibility for him. She resented this burden immensely. The stubborn, old fool refused to live in a care home – even the better quality, more expensive ones ...

After a short while, however, the Colonel's daughter would manage to block out these infuriating thoughts on her drive to work ... she deserved to block out these thoughts ... she would soon begin to sing along to the car radio once more ...

This was the ignorant bubble that the married couple lived in. Their ignorant bubble comprised only of their (1) house; (2) garden; (3) conservatory; (4) garage; (5) TV and; (6) their two cars. Nothing at all was wrong in the world. In this bubble of conspicuous consumption, they truly believed that things would just keep on getting better for them. (*They did deserve it after all!*) This was their insatiable appetite.

The day that the Colonel's daughter heard that her father had been attacked on a London tube was the day that things began to change for her – and things began to change fast. When she saw him lying in the hospital bed, so helpless, so vulnerable, her instant response was one of pure tenderness. None of her usual: 'How could he have been so stupid?' or 'How could he put me through this?' Gradually, the image of her father lying in the hospital bed made the heart of the Colonel's daughter freeze over. An ice-cold, stabbing feeling spread through her whole body. This feeling started in her heart, and spread through every vein, through every bone, into every single cell. After a couple of days, she had begun to acknowledge that her world was far from perfect … in fact, it was nowhere near perfect. She also knew that none of this was her father's fault. The iciness fought with a violent guilt, which battled through her whole body and through her mind.

That evening she sat in front of the gargantuan TV with her husband.

'Are you okay, dear?' the husband checked.

'I'm fine, darling,' the Colonel's daughter replied robotically. She had lied!

For the first time in their 25-year marriage, she had lied: she was not fine. 'This life is not fine! This world is not fine!' she thought. She did not look at her wedding picture once that night, for, no matter where she looked, all she could see was her father's vividly battered face. When she visited him again, the iciness spread over her even thicker and faster.

Still further.

A fortnight after the Prime Minister made his announcement, her husband was still crying uncontrollably. He cried like a baby for five hours solid each and every day. His family was going to lose everything – everything that they had ever worked for. Their savings, their house, their garden, their conservatory, their garage, their TV, their two cars and their coffee-making machine. Despairingly, he turned to his wife in his hour of need.

The Colonel's daughter could bear it no longer. She simply turned her back on her husband, and walked away from him. 'Stop being such a weakling!' she thought to herself.

'Dear, where are you going?' sobbed the husband, … 'Darling? DARLING?!'

Deep down, everything in her life had already gone. It had already lost meaning. How ridiculous her husband seemed at that moment! In that moment, it was her dead father – her strong and courageous father – whom she wanted to comfort so, so much … and to embrace.

But it was too late.

For the first time in her life, she was truly her father's daughter. She had to get away from her pathetic, sobbing husband immediately, or she would suffocate! She would forever suffocate from a mixture of her fumbling husband and the permanently haunting smell of cruelty that had invaded her nostrils since holding her father's cold, lifeless hand. To escape now was her only means of self-preservation.

10

He that wishes to see his country robbed
of its rights cannot be a patriot.
Samuel Johnson

The world was angry with Britain. Furious, in fact. All countries were dealing with economic collapse, travel chaos and the
prospect of mass immigration. The fundamental difference
between Britain and the rest of the world, however, was that
the rest of the world had somebody to blame for this incomprehensible disaster. The people of Britain looked to their Prime
Minister for more words of encouragement and support, but
he had disappeared off the face of the earth. Or so it seemed.
In the Prime Minister's absence, the people of Britain looked
to their Queen for reassurance, but she no longer spoke. She
just polished her crown jewels for eight hours a day in preparation for 'the sinking'. (*A queen has been taken by a pawn.*) So,
the people of Britain were lost and friendless. They had no
one. They would have to face this angry world all by themselves, confused, isolated, weak and leaderless.

In an army barracks just outside Newcastle-upon-Tyne, a
confused regiment had recently returned from the Middle East.
All British soldiers around the world had been ordered back
to their home country immediately to help man the national
state of emergency. After a few weeks, martial law had been

51

declared by the Commander-in-Chief of the Army, and the military's power and authority subsequently began to grow. An ambitious Lieutenant was amongst the returning troops.

Little was known of the Lieutenant when he had joined the Army eleven years earlier at the age of 16 – no one knew who his family or friends were, no one knew where he had attended school. All people knew was that he was a fan of Nietzsche. Despite this air of mystery, he had been successful in casting a deep impression on his comrades and superiors during the latter decade.

At just 16, the inexperienced recruit was sent to Northern Ireland to help still the escalating violence there. During this period, he had unbelievably dismantled a bomb, which would, no doubt, have killed hundreds of innocent civilians. Asked why he didn't wait for the bomb squadron to turn up, the youth had simply and matter-of-factly stated, 'They were taking too long.' (*Where he had learnt to dismantle a bomb, nobody ever found out!*) People all over the country were touched by the teenager's selfless act in saving the lives of those innocent civilians. He received an award for his quick thinking and he simultaneously shook hands with maturity. He was thus promoted to the rank of Lance Corporal.

At 19 years old, the young man was sent to the Middle East. Here, the Lance Corporal stunned his comrades once more with his outrageously brave actions. When ten enemy guerrilla soldiers kidnapped five of his comrades, he walked coolly over to the truck, and knocked each of the enemy soldiers out. Bullets shot at him from every direction, but, somehow, godlike, he managed to dodge them. The guerrilla soldiers soon gave up on their guns, and used their fists: their punches did not even penetrate the superhuman soldier, whose body seemed to be made of steel. All five soldiers were returned to camp safe, well and grateful. (*Where he had learnt to fight like that, nobody ever found out!*) At this time, the young Lance Corporal received a medal for his courageous actions, and was promoted to the rank of Corporal. Every soldier in the British Army longed to fight alongside the now legendary Corporal, for they knew that, if they were close to him, their safety was virtually guaranteed.

At 24 years old, the well-known Corporal had been deployed to a neighbouring country in the Middle East. He cemented his place in the history books during this period. One stifling night, the fast-rising star dreamt that the enemy had fired a missile at the British base, killing hundreds of soldiers. In his dream, he felt angry. He marched outside, while all the other soldiers, undisturbed, slept like babies. When the missile hurtled down from the starlit sky, the brave soldier somehow caught it using only his bare hands. He walked to the boundaries of the nearest town and, with great ease, threw it in that very direction, and from a great distance. In his vivid dream, the deafening impact could be heard more than one thousand miles away. The small town had been totally consumed by roaring flames. Mesmerised and at a distance, the Corporal had watched this spectacle: *he* had done all this, he thought to himself. He must surely be some kind of god! The acrobatic flames looked simply beautiful.

On awakening the following day, the Corporal warned his superiors of an impending missile attack.

'What evidence do you have of this?' the Commander asked, entranced.

'I know that this will happen exactly as I have foretold it. You must act with haste!'

Hypnotised by the Corporal's determined glare, the Commander took the necessary precautions without further question. The superior could not explain why he had total confidence in this young man. He just did.

That night the British Army shot down an enemy plane. The leaders on the plane had, for months, been secretly helping to plan this highly sophisticated missile attack. With incomprehensible speed, the plane plummeted down into the very centre of a small town. Hundreds of innocent civilians were killed that night. Their screams were audible amongst the flames. However, the young Corporal's one thought that night was that the flames were simply beautiful – in that moment, the deafening screams did not even detract from their perfect beauty. The celebrated hero received the Military Cross for his quick thinking and, in the months that followed, was speedily promoted through the ranks, to become a Lieutenant. This young officer was, by now, convinced of his destiny: he was to become a godlike leader … his country's Saviour! The most recent promotion had only served to confirm the gut feeling that had already been spreading through the Lieutenant's each and every vein. This new, powerful spurt of self-belief directly coincided with the Prime Minister's dramatic speech to the nation in October 2013. How strange it was for the determined Lieutenant to find himself unexpectedly on English soil once more!

The Lieutenant's regiment was given the task of maintaining order in Newcastle: on a daily basis, the Lieutenant would deploy his troops to stand guard over the queues at the petrol stations, the supermarkets, and the airports. He was bored. Very bored. A resentment began to take hold of him – this international crisis meant he couldn't fight in battle any more, he couldn't represent his country, he couldn't win more medals, he couldn't astound people with his heroic actions and cool head and, most importantly, he would not be able to follow his destiny. All the things that he had been born to do were being speedily snatched away from him. It seemed that there was absolutely nothing he could do about it. He was meant for greater things than this! The Lieutenant only sought glory and recognition, and, in these unsettled weeks, he had had plenty of time to think. During this time, he had reached one firm, solid conclusion: he was invincible.

One wintry day, the Lieutenant made a request that his comrades secretly meet him at the Angel of the North. They were instructed to meet him there that very night. The Lieutenant was very well respected, and so, when he made this request, there was a good turn-out, despite the bitterly cold wind and the heavy rain. It was a *very* good turn-out indeed. Every man – and one woman – listened intently to their hero:

'Comrades, friends, woman. I have called you here tonight to take action. Before our very eyes, our friends and families are being separated, and are already being forced to leave England. We are to be scattered across this globe like ashes in the wind. Why should this be? We are a great nation. We are the greatest nation in fact! We are England. Through history, we have always led other countries and, through history, we have always been the happy guardian of other countries. We have forever been strong. We have forever been England. I say, we are still that same England. *(There were passionate grunts of approval at this point.)* It is our destiny that we remain a strong country – that we lead the way for others.'

'What can we do Lieutenant?'

'How can we serve you?'

'Please let us serve you. Let us follow your every command. Let us hang on your every word … please … we implore you!'

'I thank you for your unfailing support – when the time is

right, I guarantee that you will be well rewarded for such stead-
fast loyalty. I will tell you what we can do … What we will do.
It is certainly true that there is nothing we can do for our fast-
sinking land. That is a fact. But of what importance is the
land anyway? It's the people – the nation – that really counts.
We will take another land. We will take another land for our
own … We will settle together as one. This is, after all, our
right as a nation! We will settle together in France! We are
destined to create our own "Little England" in France … and
our community will take over power in government to ensure
that this happens. We will always remain together as one nation!'
  (Gasps – some excited, some desperate, only a couple horrified.)
'Can it be done, Lieutenant? Can it really be done?'
'Is it really possible, our Leader?'
'How can we make it happen, Oh Mighty One?'
'Of course it's possible,' snapped the Lieutenant. 'Anything's
possible … don't let me ever hear anything different from any
of you. I, warlike by nature, am invincible. We, therefore, are
all invincible … untouchable. Only great things await us. Glory
is only ever within an arm's length.' (*Where he had learnt to make
speeches such as that, nobody ever found out.*)
  And so, for several hours, the Lieutenant's idea was planned
out and developed. Detail was added. The body of the operation was refined. Everybody who was present that night left
the meeting truly believing that great things awaited each and
every one of them. Everyone truly believed that glory was only
an arm's length away. Everyone truly believed that they, together,
would be residing in their own 'Little England' very, very soon.
For the Lieutenant had said it was so. And so it was so.

11

England expects that every man will do his duty.
Horatio Nelson

The following night, the Lieutenant was standing before the populations of Newcastle and its surrounding towns. People had walked many miles to come and see their new leader in person. Without doubt, he had magically touched the hearts of the English citizens when they had listened to his eloquent speech. They cried now – but these were new tears of joy, intermingled with tears of optimism. No tears of sadness and anxiety were shed that night, for the Lieutenant offered the people hope for the future, where they had, until then, only suffered emptiness. He offered his people warmth, where there had, until then, only been ice. They were ready to protect their precious heritage … to protect their new-found culture. The crowds were ready to claim their right to their own province. They were ready to lay down at the feet of the Lieutenant in complete and utter awe. They were England. In celebration of the certain future in prospect, and in celebration of the new wave of optimism that had swept through the crowd, a celebratory firework display was held. The crowd gasped at its beauty. The colours, the patterns, the combinations … it was all breathtaking. Too breathtaking.

'The next time we shall see such wondrous fireworks will be

when we have stepped onto … and christened … England's new soil.'

The Lieutenant's words penetrated the ears of the crowd. They started to slowly call out in a mass orgy. Crescendo.

'Come, follow me. Bring warm clothing, bring food, bring weapons … you may well need to defend yourselves and our cause. Today we become comrades. We are all the same person now. We are England.'

The country's entire transport network had, by then, crashed, apart from the continuous outward journeys that still were relentlessly taking people to their newly assigned countries. There were no normal train services, no buses (only frantic coaches to airports) – the last supplies of petrol had been shipped in weeks ago, which meant that, gradually, fewer and fewer cars were seen on the roads. The Lieutenant, therefore, marched with his people. He marched the crowd past the Angel of the North, sweeping up more support along the way. They took to the streets of Leeds, where they could not help but capture the hearts and minds of Leeds' residents. Impassioned women grabbed saucepans to use in battle. Impassioned men grabbed hammers, screwdrivers and kitchen knives. The marching snake grew. Manchester felt the March's heartbeat next, and all manner of people took up arms and joined the crowd hopefully. The people of Sheffield stood mesmerised, as the Lieutenant's newly formed army paraded through the streets of their city. Hypnotised, they could do nothing but follow. Nottingham Castle came to life once more as it stood captivated and confident in the presence of the crowd and this formidable new Robin Hood figure. The people of Nottingham excitedly joined the back of the crowd. Even the Sheriff packed up shop. (*It was here, that the Colonel's two grandsons, the law under-graduate and the mathematics student, joined up as well, with an animal-*

58

like look in their crazed eyes.) The residents of Leicester were waiting ready before the Lieutenant's army had even set foot in the city. Much of Coventry had been destroyed during World War II – its residents were not going to be destroyed again. They readily joined the march. Oxford came to life as the march wound its way through the city. Impassioned students ran to join the army. Their eyes were ablaze in the same way that the Lieutenant's eyes had been at their age, for this was the first time they had truly come to life. The Lieutenant's megalomaniacal eyes were now, however, devilish, power-hungry and frenzied. In the days that followed, this army marched on, ever stronger.

By the time they had reached the capital, it had begun to snow heavily. The monstrous crowd marched through Hyde Park, where a man and his dog joined up – the dog's barks resonated through the mass of people, determined and inspiring. They marched through the Olympic stadium, where the Lieutenant held an Olympic-style beacon for effect. It worked. (*He, who usually loathed southerners, was charming the cockney pants off them on this snow-frosted night!*) The Olympic flame blazed with fiery hope against the sparkling, crystal cityscape. They marched through Covent Garden, where various street performers joined the army eagerly. They never ceased to juggle flames and swallow fire as they proceeded. Then on to Trafalgar Square, where, for the first time in history, the crowd managed to scare the pigeons away. (*Incidentally, the terrified birds never returned.*) Tower Bridge just about coped with the mass of citizens who pounded over it with a fierce, burning passion.

It is here that the banker joined the historical march. Even William J. Smith – usually so monotone – managed to energise the tiring, cold crowd with his enthusiastic chants. He felt alive. He felt wide awake. His excited heart pounded hard and the sweat trickled down his red forehead with a new kind of venom. He desperately tried to catch a glimpse of the Lieutenant in the flesh. Anytime that an opportunity presented itself, he would push men, women and even young children out of the way to try and make this new dream of his a reality. To date though, he had been unsuccessful in managing to catch a glimpse of his hero. Despite this, the thought that the Lieutenant was in the vicinity kept the momentum ticking powerfully and inspirationally within William's heart.

When the Lieutenant's army arrived at Canterbury Cathedral, the Archbishop joined the back, waving his right fist in the air with conviction. He carried an archaic, flaming baton in the other. (*He was certainly not going to be suppressed as Becket had been centuries earlier. Not he!*) The White Cliffs of Dover shook as the people marched through the town. Ominously, colossal lumps of chalk crashed down on to the shores below. Thousands of fish were washed up on to the shore the next day; chalk solidified their once slimy mouths. By the time the Lieutenant's army had finally reached its destination – the Channel Tunnel at Cheriton – the crowd was five million strong. Every one huddled up to one another and slept. Many people never woke up, for they had not realised how cold their bodies actually were, such was the surge of their euphoric feelings. Euphoria could not warm their bodies back to life though, and rats and flies now danced together over their inert carcasses.

When the crowd finally began to stir, the Lieutenant sadistically ordered the people nearest the front to scoop the snow out of the tunnel's entrance with their bare hands – the tunnel had not been used for some weeks now, and its maintenance had been neglected. Reluctantly, the crowd began to follow his instructions. (*Incidentally, when later asked why men, women and children had lost their fingers to frostbite, witnesses, including William, guiltily denied all knowledge of this order. They were guilty of witnessing it, for they had done nothing. If the truth be known, it had only succeeded in exciting them still further.*) Some hours later, the crowd began to march through the Channel Tunnel. Their hearts were ablaze, for, unfailingly, the Lieutenant had worked them up into an impassioned frenzy once more. He did it so easily.

Having recently learnt that the breathing tunnel was being penetrated once more, French policeman made their way cautiously into its entrance. In the centre of the tunnel, hundreds of the English collided with hundreds of French policemen. (*Ironically, they met at the very point in the tunnel where French and English tunnel constructors had famously shaken hands over two decades earlier. New enemies began to savagely kill one another now.*) Unprepared, the French policemen were soon defeated, most having been suffocated in the squash against the tunnel's walls.

Awareness heightened, William clambered over the bodies. Shock hit him, as he saw the glazed eyes of the dead French staring up at him, statue-still. For a second, he was unable to breathe. Unable to blink. The putrid, fleshy smell snatched at his nostrils and lingered within him for several hours. In spite of himself, he continued his journey through the dark tunnel. Soon, however, the crazy crowd was just trampling obliviously on these bodies. By the time the last of the English had gone through the tunnel, the French bodies were squashed flat on the floor of the tunnel. The only evidence of them ever being there was the blood that had crimsoned all the surface of the ground and walls. Hundreds of pairs of French eyes somehow though remained perfectly intact, even though each body had been completely maimed and flattened. The clear eyes stared eternally hard into the face of sin that had mercilessly over-powered them. In the future weeks, these eyes could not be removed, no matter how hard the walls and floors were scrubbed. When England sank, the tunnel disappeared, deeper still into the seabed. But still French eyes looked upwards, judgingly and relentlessly. William had seen these eyes and felt the full, terrifying power that their Judgment Day expression held:

'William, look what you've done! How could you do this to us? How could you do this to yourself?'

He had carried on walking forward nonetheless.

12

I know my fate. One day there will be
associated with my name the recollection of something frightful.
Of a crisis like no other before on earth, of the profoundest collision of
conscience, of a decision evoked against everything that until then had been
believed in, demanded, sanctified.
I am not a man, I am dynamite.

Friedrich Nietzsche

The Lieutenant and the English now had to work fast if they were going to reach their new, desired province, which was just south of Paris. They needed to take control of the capital first, so as to ensure political influence. The French had already begun to mobilise. The first priority of the Lieutenant was to pass through Calais. The leader led the groups through the path of houses and numerous hypermarkets. The sheer mass of the English against the unprepared citizens of Calais meant that the English passed through Calais 'easily and smoothly'. Only a few English died defending themselves from fuming residents. It mattered not to the Lieutenant that several residents of Calais had been killed in the bloodbath.

Next, the Lieutenant's still massive army passed through Arras, Amiens and Reims without 'too much fuss' … only ten more English fatalities to add to the list. Things were going well. Very well. If everything went according to plan, the English would be sipping tea in their new 'Little England' within the week. Firstly, however, one, simple fact remained: the Lieutenant's army would need to take control of Paris success-fully. This did not worry the leader in the least, for he knew that he was invincible. He was a living legend, and his status was ever-expanding.

On the day that the Lieutenant's gargantuan army finally entered Paris, they marched through from the north-west of the town. Following their leader, millions marched through the Arc de Triomphe. A large group was ordered to take the Eiffel Tower, so that they could oversee all the action. They waved and laughed at the devastated Parisians from the heights of the classic monument. Only 20 French and 15 English had been killed in this initial movement. A second group were told to temporarily seize Notre Dame in order to stun the Parisians still further.

And so, William J. Smith and his comrades ran through the cathedral like a thousand Quasimodos. A mere 15 French guards were killed – William had killed one of these guards. With a single blow, he had taken the man from behind and hit him on the head with an iron hammer. No guilt was experienced by him in this moment – only utterly inspired exhilaration. But then, he saw the victim's shocked eyes staring back at him. His comrade called his name, but he could not withdraw from the man's shiny stare. He sat by the inert body and brushed his hand against the stranger's cheek. All of a sudden, the victim's head turned violently round. The carcass's head lifted itself up, so as to look even deeper into William's eyes. Petrified, William dropped the victim's hand and sprinted off to rejoin his group. He leaned against a stone wall to recover. In that moment, he was convinced he saw the wall breathing in and out too, anxiously and guiltily.

'How could you do this William?' Again, the same dismayed voice resonated into his ear.

William covered both his ears in shock at the severity of a sudden case of ear-ache. He soon learnt that only 7 English men and women had died in this particular confrontation. On learning this, the remaining English fighters cuddled and kissed one another in celebration of their small victory. All except William, who, at that moment, was experiencing acute pain. Many wandering Parisians were crying out, desperately confused, in the capital's streets; most, however, ran to their homes to take cover.

The third main group of English soldiers was ordered to take the lift up to the top of the Montparnasse Tower, and to watch the city of Paris 'like hawks'. They began to relax and smile after a while though, for things were going according to plan ... perfectly. The Louvre, the Panthéon and the Opera House were all taken efficiently and with minimal bloodshed. '*Très bien*,' spat the Lieutenant insolently. He was pleased. This was all too easy. The Eiffel Tower shimmered beautifully that night. 'That's for us,' thought the leader contently. 'That's for England ... for "Little England". That's for me.'

With the Parisians hidden away, Paris belonged to the English that night. They ate the abandoned food in Michelin five-star restaurants, sharing the company of the night's first stars. The food tasted delicious, even though it had gone cold. William tried to join in the celebrations. He popped open a bottle of chilled champagne in one of the deserted, continental bars, and forced a smile towards the people he shared company with. However, his ears still were causing him agonising pain, and he could still see the judging eyes of his victim, no matter which way he turned. William noticed that others seemed totally oblivious to this moral carnage.

Husbands continued to serenade their tired, exhausted wives. Children giggled happily in the presence of this loving spectacle. 'How she fought today, armed only with a wooden spoon,' the husbands would think to themselves. Looking into the playful, happy eyes of their husbands, the wives would think, 'How brave my husband was in the line of duty. He has served his country well today. He has defended the rights of our nation heroically. I am proud of him!' English men playfully danced with one another that night. Many heterosexual men, for the first time, acknowledged that the gay patriots were, indeed, real men too. They toasted each friend for their personal contribution to this historic victory. Tomorrow, when they finally reached their province, they would, together, go down in the history books as the army that saved the English nation. (*Surely, the greatest army of all time too!*) They had given England new life in this strange new world. Oh, wonderful England – a new land of hope and glory! How they all loved each other that night, and how they all loved their country. (*For many of them, this was the first time they had experienced genuine love for their country – until then, their lives had been totally unpatriotic.*)

All of the English, without exception, fell asleep, safely and in warmth that night. Exhausted, they snuggled up together with smiles fixed on their faces. The new life that they were in the process of creating for themselves was only a few miles away. It was within arm's length now. Reincarnation … a new beginning for them, and a new beginning for generations to come.

Stomp, stomp, stomp, stomp, stomp, stomp, STOMP, STOMP, STOMP, STOMP.
(*The sleeping English stirred.*)
STOMP, STOMP, STOMP, STOMP.

Early the next morning, the English were awakened by the sound of marching. The marching was angry and authoritative. The marching was immense and beyond all comprehensible human proportions. Their senses heightened, the invaders sat up in alarm – they had been awoken so abruptly from their happy dreams. A message was broadcast to them from a loud speaker in the centre of the capital:

'This is the Head of the French Army addressing you. The *whole* French Army has now arrived in Paris. We have arrived to reclaim our capital. You had no right to come here ... What were you thinking?! ... It was delusional. You have one hour to make your way back to the Arc de Triomphe. If you follow this order, you will escape with your lives. If you choose to disobey, you will certainly die.'

Sheer panic launched itself amongst the, now awake, English. This was an infectious panic and an infectious reality check. Men, woman and children began to scream in terror. In that moment, there took place a rapid and an extreme u-turn.

'We must follow their orders.'

'We can't risk our lives. We can't die. We must protect our families!'

'We should never have come. Why did we ever listen to him? Did he ever really speak to our souls?' William asked himself these questions in stupid disbelief. All colour had drained from his face. He felt as empty as a drum inside. The pain was still ringing through his ears and his brain, as he now faced the very real prospect of imprisonment.

Most of the English immediately took the decision to peacefully comply with French orders. (*Men of the Colonel's generation would have fought on, but this was a different era.*) All too quickly they had realised how ridiculously illogical they had been in recent weeks. They had been hypnotised, though. The men now reminded themselves that they had a responsibility to their wives, and the wives now reminded themselves that they had a responsibility to their children. The children now reminded themselves that they had a responsibility to their teddy-bears and dolls. They began to walk to the Arc de Triomphe slowly, silently. They walked with their heads down. A dramatic wave of embarrassment suddenly swept over them, as the bitter Parisians stared at them out of their picturesque windows. The natives threw things at them. Enraged, an elderly French lady spat at William and shouted in his face *(for once, she and her fellow country men and women could not be bothered to speak English, and so most of this torrent of abuse passed untranslated. The tone was perfectly understandable to William though. It required no translation whatsoever!)*

Witness to the English surrender, the Lieutenant, for the first time, seemed to fall into a blind panic. He ran beside the train of English people, screaming into their ears. But it was as if he was now invisible to them.

'You can't let them win. You can't give up so pathetically. We are invincible.'

His spell was broken though, and the English walked on. The Lieutenant looked undignified and pathetic – William saw just how pathetic the man that he, until so recently, had hero-worshipped, had now become. *(Reality shocked William. Reality shook him hard. It laughed harshly in his ruby face. It sniggered spittingly at his defeat. It also tittered at his ignorance: to successfully overcome by force will only ever defeat half of your enemy anyway … How could William not have known that?)*

The English gave themselves up peacefully at the Arc de Triomphe. They were ashamed of themselves, and they were indescribably embarrassed. They were placed into French prisons all over the country immediately. *(Such was the demand on the French prison service, that new, haphazard buildings needed to be erected very quickly.*) All too soon, William found himself in a dingy prison on the outskirts of the capital.

One man, however, did not give himself up. The Lieutenant manically made his way up to the top of the Eiffel Tower and looked out over the whole of Paris.

'You'll never take me. I'm invincible. I am England!' he screamed out. But, in his manic call, a seed of uncertainty had been sewn and was easily detectable. In a split second, the energy within him suddenly contracted. His disintegrating call echoed around the capital and scraped the ears of millions.

… A moment later, France's leading sniper shot him in the head with ease, and then coolly lit up a cigarette.

13

Be England what she will.
With all her faults, she is my country still.
                                        Charles Churchill

Frenzied panic sets in fast. An accelerating desperation leaps eerily onto a global stage. Darkness ensues: darkness of the mind and darkness of the future. Deafening screams strangle silent screams; silent screams strangle deafening screams (*it's impossible to distinguish between the two any more*). Culture's foot is caught in deathly, cruel seaweed. Tangling. Tangled. Aqua nature pulls civilisation down into its eerie depths.

Culture screams out, 'Do you know who I am? Can you contemplate the magnitude of my achievements? I gave birth to Shakespeare. I nurtured Elizabeth's Golden Age. I brought up Britannia as my own. I possess centuries of credibility. Do not pull me down, Poseidon … I command that you do not pull me down!'

Alas, Poseidon's power is limitless. The human mind can never comprehend, nor understand, limitless power. Mother Nature's decisions will always come to pass, challenged or unchallenged. Defeated and pale, Culture turns her head from the light and looks down to the dark, freezing sea-bed. (*With dignity, Milton witnesses everything, and he knowingly sees Culture lying before him.*) And so, Culture finally accepts her watery end. She

70

never thought that she would taste salty, suffocating mortality. Not she! The coldness bites at her body like one thousand starving piranhas. She screams out. The scream travels through the world's oceans with lightning speed. As it picks up speed, giant waves penetrate foreign lands. No kindly ears hear the scream – in fact, the scream's massive tsunami only serves to increase global hostility. It only increases the contempt felt towards the British people. *('The tsunami has caused even more devastation, when we already needed to deal with so much! The English are to blame for all of this.')*

Culture is now silent, it's carcass preserved only in the memories of its children. An eerie, titanic shell. A half-life whispers deep in the minds of the British people.

The Queen's eyes shut gracefully. The flapping of birds' wings breaks the agonising silence.

From the moment Paradise became tainted, problems have always arisen ... obstacles have always been encountered ...

A banker had a dream one night, so vivid and so real, that it was much more than just a dream – for never had he experienced such faultless clarity when awake. He dreamt of a golden city, the splendour and spiritual perfection of which was beyond all human comprehension – only in a dream was it possible to understand and experience its full, translucent beauty ... only on angels' wings. Humans lived together peacefully under Atlantis' rule. They had developed the faculties of Art and Science. These humans were so weirdly beautiful that they simply had to be a unique race ... a legendary race. Mystic tribes.

The encapsulated moment was thousands of years past, but yet somehow, it also represented the future. Timeless. Too perfect ...

Human weakness then set in. Mortal mistakes. Mortal greed. Fighting. Vandalism. Poseidon awoke from his deep slumber.

He arose to the water's surface fiercely, and saw his perfect creation ruined. He was angry – his breath sent chilling shivers racing manically through the island. A single, golden trident can cause human catastrophe. The golden city began to suddenly sink under a gargantuan tidal wave. Deafening screams. Heartstopping hysteria. Eternal disappearance. The sea stole Atlantis' remaining treasures scornfully. The waves cruelly enveloped Atlantis' beautiful artwork punishingly. The irate ocean took Atlantis' new knowledge in one violent, laughing gush. The lost city sank, deep down, to the pitch black ocean bed.

… England sank, deep down, to the pitch black ocean bed. Deep down into the freezing cold, leaving only traces of Culture's whispers in the harshly naive world above … whispers of a magnificent English heritage ... only echoes and whispers. Mythology now … reality no more … stirring …

… the people's remorseful tears still ride the waves senselessly …

He's stirring now …

Dream's metamorphosis. Spiralling tunnels. Time has so little meaning within eternity…

He's stirring …

Physical dimensions have never had significance in the microscopic and macroscopic non-limits of The All.

'I awake. Raging torrents of water envelop me. I am here living the event, and I'm in such close proximity to the raging waters.'

(*The human soul has always striven for intensity over happiness.*)

'Awareness of the immense power of the rushing water hits me instantly. I know that nothing in its path can survive its limitless threat.'

'Oh, wake me up … Please, Lord, wake me up from this!

Part Three

14

Signior Antonio, many a time and oft
In the Rialto you have rated me
About my moneys and my usances:
Still have I borne it with a patient shrug;
For sufferance is the badge of all our tribe.
You call me misbeliever, cut-throat dog,
And spit upon my Jewish gaberdine,
And all for use of that which is mine own.
Well then, it now appears you need my help:
Go to, then; you come to me, and you say
'Shylock, we would have moneys': you say so;
You, that did void your rheum upon my beard,
And foot me as you spurn a stranger cur
Over your threshold: moneys is your suit.
What should I say to you? Should I not say
'Hath a dog money? Is it possible
A cur can lend three thousand ducats?' or
Shall I bend low and in a bondman's key,
With bated breath and whispering humbleness,
Say this, -
'Fair sir, you spit on me on Wednesday last;
You spurn'd me such a day; another time
You call'd me dog, and for these courtesies
I'll lend you thus much moneys'?

Shylock, *The Merchant of Venice*,
William Shakespeare

Decades passed. The decades breathed with difficulty for the English. Asthmatic inhalations. Thousands of English persecuted just for being English. Thousands of Englishmen tortured in the world's vicious circus. This resource-sucking race possessed complete responsibility for all of the world's extreme economic difficulties. In the Southern States, an elderly English citizen, of Caribbean descent, was crucified on a makeshift cross one night. He was crucified in star-glazed woods for trying to spread a message of humility and love through his new community. (*Afterwards, these very same natives became angry that two of their own trees had been wasted on him ... they had been wasted on 'another English sponger'.*)

'They have sucked the blood out of us like leeches ... dirty leeches. Every one of the leechy scum is to blame for our problems. Every single one of them. Why should we suffer for them? We'll teach them a lesson ... a lesson that we will never allow them to forget. How dare they impose themselves upon us in this way!'

This was the global mindset, and it only grew haphazardly stronger with each passing day.

Pain.

Imprisonment.

Torture.

Mockery.

Humiliation.

Disgrace.

Punishment.

The months that William had spent in captivity had been draining and hard. When, at last, he walked out of the prison, he was hopelessly thin and pale.

'Where can I go?' William initially asked himself.

However, several months following his release, the answer to this heart-wrenching question was all too evident for him. He now told himself:

'I have nowhere to go. Everything I once had is now gone. Everything has disappeared into dust ... even my pride and self-respect. All is grass – even my soul.'

And so, the dispersed nation had no choice but to stay in their newly designated countries. And the early years were sharp and hard-hitting ... as sharp as a brand-new blade. The nation no longer walked with their heads optimistically high ... they no longer walked with the twinkle of Britannia in their eyes. Instead, the nation looked at their feet as, dirtily, they roamed foreign streets: the last thing they wanted to do was to make eye contact with anyone and exacerbate the situation still further ... they knew that they would only suffer for that in the long run! As individual eyes focused on individual foot-steps, individual shoulders became hunched and despondent. As individual shoulders became hunched and despondent, individual voices grew weaker, quieter and even more frightened. A nation that, in past decades, could not be intimidated, now jumped whenever spoken to. Natives scornfully would scream, 'You sponging English ... jump into the sea. Go find your own land!' A once fearless nation was now being forced into accepting the spit that lingered on their shoes, and it became William's preferred choice to look at this phlegm, rather than to look up into an endless sea of hateful, crazed eyes. (*Kind gestures and loving, sympathetic eyes were offered by a tiny minority only.*)

So as to be made easily identifiable, it became law in many countries that the English needed to sew the St. George's flag upon their clothes. (*And what is a flag anyway? Is it the symbolisation of a nation or the nationalisation of a symbol? Does the flag own the country or does the country own the flag?*)

It mattered not for the English: this branding became the

law, and if you chose to break the law, death would follow. The English were pushed over at the whim of foreigners. They were pushed into putrid puddles. Putrid humanity. If they wore the badge, they were not given access to the same places as the natives. (*History, no doubt, is cyclical.*)

... only in their dreams, did the English allow themselves to remember their past lives. Only in their dreams did they hear Culture's sad, honest whisperings reach up, deep from the ocean bed:

'Do you remember me? Can you still feel my passion? Do you remember my greatness?' she would whisper in a melancholy, lost tone.

'What is true greatness?' the English nation would now reply dejectedly.

Some dreamt of warm, hearty meals. Others dreamt of parties and fashion. Some survivors dreamt of season tickets and local pubs. Others dreamt of studying ... they dreamt of their past, and of so many naive hopes for the future. Others dreamt of the sea, and some dreamt of the buildings. Some smelt the fish markets. Others smelt the farms. The once rich allowed themselves to dream of the Opera House and fast cars. The ever poor pondered over the financial support they used to receive from the Government. (*How they had taken it for granted then!*)

William usually dreamt of his flat and his brown leather sofa. He could still feel the comforting coolness of it on his skin, even as he slept. The sensation was almost comforting enough to momentarily extinguish his pain. Almost. His hearing permanently damaged, William also enjoyed the familiar, warm sounds of his old laptop in his dreams, and he would very occasionally smile in his sleep at the affectionate, beeping sounds. He also dreamt of his friends, who, it is true, had not played a significant part in his past life ... he now held on to the memory of their vivid, gleaming smiles. He now felt their tangible, reassuring warmth reaching out to him. And then he would awake ...

Dark loneliness and cruel fortune clung on to one another desperately when William stirred.

The nation was a shadow of its former self, with not even the energy to cry anymore. No more tears to give or to share. There only existed empty depression. The desire to be released by death was coupled with the basic human instinct to survive, and, here, there existed a tension. Culture's ghostly fingers caressed her children one by one, so that they could sleep some more ... so that they could remember just a little bit more ...

Eventually most of the English stopped themselves from dreaming, as it hurt too much. Now, in complete and utter isolation, the only experience that existed for them was loneliness, even as they slept.

William still dreamt though, and his dreams sometimes took hold of him with a vivacity and energy all of their own ...

Two fishermen had been rowing tirelessly. For days they had seen only water. For days they had inhaled only the sea-salt air. Their cheeks were cold and their skin had become pale.

A small island – which had seemed like only a dot to begin with – was gradually getting bigger, as the father and son rowed closer and closer towards it. In awe of its magnificence, their eyes were naturally drawn to the classical church that dominated the whole landscape. Surrounded by archaic houses and walls, the church stood proudly and authoritatively. Its spire was the highest point of the island by far, and its tip really did seem to touch the pink heavens above. A faint moon smiled naively. It was a timeless image.

In a very short space of time, however, dark clouds threateningly invaded the pink skies. *(William shuddered in his sleep.)* The two men knew, in this moment, that they were running out of time. All at once, their small boat had begun to rock more violently. Concerned, the son took the glass jar out from inside his fleecy, green jacket. He stared down at it, and was reassured by the stunning glow, which danced around within the confines of the glass. The purple light reflected outwards and lit up the son's jade-green eyes. He stroked it lovingly. The fishermen docked their wooden boat in the small harbour, and quickly began their ascent up the steep, cobbled road. The island seemed to be totally deserted. Up and up they climbed. A tremendous roll of thunder suddenly overpowered them, as a flash of lightning frighteningly lit up the whole town.

'We're going to be too late,' whispered the father under his breath. *(William somehow understood the meaning of the words all too clearly.)*

The son had overheard his father's utterance and, for a second, felt discouraged. Then the beautiful, waltzing lights from within the jar caught his eye, and he felt a wave of optimism rush through him once more. He encouraged his father to continue along their path.

On entering the church, the two men looked around and immediately found the dark, spiral staircase that led up to the golden spire. Gasping for breath, they took the stairs two at a time, as the thunder's war cry grew even louder. It sounded so angry. When they finally reached the small, round room, the father suddenly held his chest for, in that moment, a tight pain had taken hold of him. The son stared at him with a look of empathetic terror. He knelt down by his father and kissed him on the cheek. His father nodded knowingly at his child.

80

With the glass jar in his coat, the young man climbed out of the window and began to negotiate his way to the tip of the spire. He used all of his remaining strength to pull himself up, while the thunder bellowed laughingly around him. The storm teased the son, as it prepared itself for its ultimate moment. Finally, at the highest point of the whole landscape, the son took the glass jar out of his coat with his free hand. Just as the lightning hit the golden spire, the son unscrewed the lid. He fell silently down to the road beneath. Bright purple light filled the sky. It was beautiful. The storm stopped instantly.

The angel, who the son had released, sadly looked down at the small, inert figure beneath. She gracefully blinked. The holy figure then looked up and joined a thousand pairs of soft, mighty wings in a heavenly embrace. A radiant spirit had been set free from captivity, and the fishermen could now row their boat in an eternal wave of peace.

For the first time in several months, William smiled in his sleep.

15

Confusion heard his voice, and wild uproar
Stood ruled, stood vast infinitude confined;
Till at his second bidding darkness fled,
Light shone, and order from disorder sprung.
                                        John Milton

And so time passed.

Years turned into two decades. A freezing half-death at first.
Yet, over time, the English began to look into one another's
eyes and see brothers and sisters.

Gradually.

Very slowly.

Camaraderie.

In the English flag, an abundant kinship was timidly sprouting.
The flag and the nation were kindred spirits. Neither dominated the other. Slowly and hopefully, English hearts began to
beat as one giant organ. The English in Madagascar began to
feel inexplicably close to the English in Peru. The English in
Poland began to relate to the English in Vietnam, despite the
fact that they had never even set eyes on one another.

Over time, William did not walk with his head looking at
his phlegm-encrusted shoes. He began to hold his head up
high, and, when he saw an English flag emblazoned upon a
tatty shirt, he would nod and smile knowingly at the bearer.

He or she would always nod back. A love began to flow through the dispersed nation. A closeness that had been extinguished for many centuries was gradually being reborn stronger than ever.

Twenty years earlier, England had been totally oblivious to impending disaster: she operated powerfully, and her people had possessed a land which they could call their own. They were, however, no nation. People had felt nothing but contempt for one another as they made their way to work. People only felt jealousy towards others who possessed more than them materially. Now, however, scattered in every corner of the earth, a nation was genuinely beginning to grow. And how good it felt! What warmth was this? Never had there been such a warmth within the land that was once called 'England'.

And people craved this warmth more and more. They, thus, began to meet together. They began to worship together. And so, a new religion slowly emerged: a new religion, which defined the English people, was born. This race of people were now united as one, and by one religion, and the bond between them was being continuously strengthened and reinforced. (*You cannot comprehend this pure happiness and this white love.*) Not since the battle of Catholicism and Protestantism had religion been so prevalent amongst the English race. However, this race was now fuelled by entirely positive, unitary feelings, and a new cultural energy and national identity were being born. The rest of the world watched on. (*Silently, the rest of the world watched on in tense jealously: it secretly desired the feelings of closeness that it now bore witness to. It, too, wanted to beat with one heart. However, the world would never verbalise this desire out loud, and it disguised its green face by mocking the religion and by mocking the English nation even more.*) Therefore, segregation continued to increase, and incidents of racism only grew more terrifying still.

However, foreign treatment such as this only made the nation's bond stronger, and it only made the love that existed between each person more powerful. One hundred years ago, a true Englishman had defined himself by Britannia ... by the colonial and empirical wealth, which he was able to profit from. Two decades ago, a true Englishman had defined himself by (1) his house; (2) his garden; (3) his conservatory; (4) his garage; (5) his TV and; (6) his two cars. Now these English men and English women defined themselves by the strength of the tangible love that existed between them ... only that. This mattered more than one thousand cars and one thousand houses combined ... so much more. A mass exodus of the English Soul had finally occurred, and the English cultural heart now beat stronger than it ever had done previously.

William now meditated daily. He had been forced into cleansing himself of all worldly possessions. A former student held his hand wordlessly. The sting of former England still resided faintly within her, but more tangible were her prayers of gratitude. The two never spoke. They never felt the need to: words create limitations, and their experience in the warm, buzzing silence was whole and boundless. She did, however, think back to those former years: 'Yes, Shylock had *definitely* been a victim.' She could see that now, and she smiled knowingly. Smiled at her former ignorance. Thousands of miles away, a family, whose priority had once been solely to 'keep up with the Jones', now meditated side by side daily. They were, finally, at peace, and they felt that radiant peace emanating throughout their whole bodies, throughout their whole beings, and throughout their very souls. This elderly couple had, only in recent years, experienced true love for one another. They now believed that their past feelings had been farcical, their foundations rooted only in material gain.

'Out of disaster, good will always prevail in the end', they would now tell each other. 'You just need to be patient and wait for her to turn up! You just need to place your trust in her, for she will always arrive – she'll be drawn to you all the quicker if she can feel the optimism resonating through your very soul.' (*For optimism and belief combined act as the most powerful magnet in drawing good luck to people: the more a person positively believes, the luckier that person becomes. Is this not true? The English nation now believed it to be so.*)

In the darkest of shadows dances the best of luck, and, in the face of disaster, a banker had once asked:

'Why can't I see His pair of footprints walking side-by-side with mine? I look for them, and I just can't see them!'

'Why, I was carrying you of course,' replied a now familiar, reassuring voice deep within his soul.

The voice was a holy, silent one.

The day was dawning.

'This is the cycle of creation,' the voice continued, 'Do not turn away from The Truth!'

And so, William continued to listen.

85

16

Regret you not the sins of the past,
Look forward to the time when, at last,
The Way has been trod and The Gate opens wide
For you to enter The Paradise inside.

George W. Gee

In this compulsive, magnetic tide of love, the English nation instinctively began to feel the need to meet physically with one another. They wanted to hold the hands of their sisters and they wanted to embrace their brothers. It mattered not that they were strangers. The people of England all began to experience whisperings in their souls.

The voice whispered, 'You must go there.'

The voice whispered, 'You must make your way there'.

The voice whispered, 'You must never look back.' (*Was this to be an incomprehensible pilgrimage? A mass Mecca? The Promised Land? ... The nation could not explain what this was, but they continued to unquestioningly place their trust in the voice.*)

Despite their lack of understanding or rationality, the English had complete faith in their souls' words ... complete faith in the whisperings, which always fluttered in their hearts, and complete faith in the silent wisdom which always danced through their being.

'Where should we go?' William implored silently, 'Guide us, please guide us.'

Invisible hands reached out to William warmly. Passionately and unprompted, he began to walk. The English nation all began to walk in the very same moment. They did not know where they were going, but they exuded utter spiritual confidence, for they knew that they were not alone.

'Two pairs of footprints always,' William whispered, completely at peace.

Murmurs began to flood the world. Murmurs began to dart fearfully from country to country:

'The English have begun to walk. They have not been granted permission, yet they do not look back ... They walk so confidently'.

Secretly the natives thought, 'I fear their confidence. I fear their passion. I fear their love!' (*Yet, they needn't have possessed such thoughts, for any soul has the same potential to develop as every other soul: this is progress along the Way.*)

Global news began to report a mass exodus. Headlines blasted, and television crews filmed the walking nation. And the fear grew and grew. And this fear fast gained momentum. The natives could not bear this newfound confidence, and they could not bear the unwavering strength of this love.

For months, the English nation walked over lands, and sailed across mighty seas and oceans. And, on serene days, William would stare out at the sparkling water and the gleaming horizon. In his silent world, he would slowly inhale the ultra-fresh, salty air. He softly whispered to the endless seascape:

'Why did I not notice you before? I only saw tragedy when I looked upon your waves ... but they are simply and breathtakingly beautiful. If you look closely – extremely closely – your waves pull in opposite directions at the same time. I can't believe that I never noticed this before! Look how the sun dances so seductively on the peak of each and every ripple. No two ripples are identical either … it's as if the palms of a million souls are holding hands. I think I am sailing through infinity. Am I still here? Someone please tell me if I am still here!'

A pause. A stillness.

And then, he did continue.

'If things hadn't changed, I would only have seen water when I looked upon you. Now, I see your true depths! This was all a blessing … everything I've ever been through was a blessing after all. I really do now see you in all your completion!'

A student of life turned to William, and asked:

'But, do we only see this beauty because, deep down, we know that we were not meant to be standing here today?'

William lip-read her words.

'The English were *always* meant to stand here today, in this eternal moment.' He answered her so confidently.

They were silent once more, and they were content.

And, in the very centre of that vast ocean, some of the travellers believed that they saw a lone, white bird flying confidently in the distance. And, just for a split second, William heard the graceful beating of an angel's wings. Then the perfect sound was gone … Once again, silence engulfed him.

Intimidated by the English commitment, the natives, in a hypnotic and extraordinary way, allowed entry as requested, without question and without exception. The natives provided food in abundance, as well as warm shelter. The genuinely loving glints, which existed in the depths of William's eyes, constituted his very survival. This was the case for the whole nation. And in this way, the mystical roamers were drawn ever closer to one another, and an ever strengthening bond grew. The whispers continued to sacredly guide them steadfastly and consistently, for the Way was always open to those that chose to follow the path. The path ensured the evolution of their souls, and this was now the only objective of their existence. The energy generated by this spiritual force began to define a nation, and the evolution of that very same nation took place before the mindful eyes of the world. And so, every single base-soul blossomed in a stunning wave of violet light.

William continued to listen intently to the sacred whisperings, and he kept on moving. The nation travelled onwards, ever equal ... stronger and stronger always. The road ahead was now open and the Way was now clear, for the Divine Force was eternally within him. Round the bend and into the valley, nature had given out a new mantle.

One bright day, millions of walking people finally met. And this nation finally embraced. A nation finally wept. This nation was unified perfectly in the simple beauty of the moment. Consciously or subconsciously, William had been dreaming of this moment for years now. A nation was unified by the voice that resonated during life's constant mental journey:

> *Travel safely, travel quick.*
> *My whispering mouth deafeningly out of sight.*
> *Love keeps us always bound together.*
> *This is The Way, The Truth and The Light.*
> *Have no fear of anything.*
> *Fear not angry words nor closed doors.*
> *Visualise the strength of our union*
> *And my footprints will always stride alongside yours.*

'I hear you,' replied William in a state of complete reverence and tranquil awe.

17

The mind is its own place and in itself,
can make a Heaven of Hell, a Hell of Heaven.

John Milton

Like history, everything in nature is cyclical – the seasons, the moon, the blooming of a flower. Energy cannot be destroyed. It transmutes, for life is eternal. Disappearance is an illusion, for energy always arrives somewhere else. We live in a holographic world, where the minutest portion of history's memory will be repeated on an immense scale. In the beginning, The Truth was known in The All, but then humanity fell. New cosmic vibrations were now attuning humans to a spiritual awakening. The mind began to create good through love. But, reverence, humility and eagerness required the promise of a new land …

And so, the spirit of Atlantis finally began to awaken from its deep slumber.

And portions of the land began to rise slowly. With each passing day, a new area of lush, green land would appear above the ocean's surface. (*Cayce smiled knowingly at this from his grave, for he had predicted this phenomenon over a century before.*)

The world watched mesmerised and confused:

'A new land rising from the ocean's dark abyss?' 'Atlantis' return?'

90

'How can this be possible?'

The English nation, however, continued to listen, and they now heard a new call. An effortless change beautifully occurred, as the people began to suddenly walk in a new direction.

They walked towards the rising island of Atlantis peacefully and powerfully. They walked with grace, with inner knowledge and with purity of soul towards their new land. The wisdom of the ages was imprinted in their very footprints. Their spirituality was tangible to all foreign bystanders (*who, for decades after the nation's surge, felt an emotional wave rush joyously through their minds, every time they relived their experience of witnessing a mystical race's holy steps. They felt truly privileged*).

The English walked silently and humbly, always listening. William only stopped in his journey to eat, sleep and meditate. Every now and again, his gentle voice could be heard saying:

'We're going home. We're really going home. He's answered our prayers … All I feel is happiness and love …'

And happiness and love is all that William did feel in that moment, for there was no room left within him for any other sensation.

Thousands of years ago, a nation walked between parted waves to reach their homeland. And, now, the English, reborn, arrived home too. Atlantis was reborn in both physical and spiritual planes. The legend of a British island was long lost in the mind's shadows. To this race of people, the words 'capitalism' and 'war' became examples of long-lost and unrecognisable vocabulary. The memories of victimisation and discrimination had been pushed outside the journey that had taken place within. All that remained was understanding, unity, love and knowledge, combined and in abundance.

Such godlike knowledge helped the English nation to create

a perfect land. It was a utopia, where religion, science, art and natural living were all one and the same thing. The landscape was breathtaking, and well loved by its people. The buildings were beautiful and godlike: impossibilities were engrained into all architectural foundations. Beautiful cities contained splendid, colossal buildings of white marble, many of which were embellished with gold. Methods of mining, quarrying, dressing and moving, once lost to humanity, had been rediscovered. Scholars were educated in the ways of natural living. The new laws, created by the Elders, were age old-laws and laws of creativity. Simple, faultless lives were led by all, and men and women were equals. Humans performed spiritual acts, not for sensational exhibitionism, but to contribute to their rich experience of the physical plane. Growing awareness and genuine sensitivities were latent in everyone. Higher levels were now being reached. Great advances and higher creation vibrated. Now, the forces of good enabled people, wildlife and the environment to function as they were intended to. The physical plane, in its entirety, now functioned correctly, as was meant to be. Competition of any kind was not known, and Paradise on earth reigned. Everything was in perfect order.

This was the prospect of a better future for William, and, in the distance, Britannia watched this new Golden Age totally dumbfounded and in awe; for, undisturbed, Eden-like flowers had begun to bloom once again.

18

Since the beginning, life on Earth has changed in many ways. Once, during what was called the Golden Age, the laws of Nature were observed in the natural way of life. Complete harmony existed between all of the different species of life on Earth, for the well being of the perfect environment was a prime and natural function. There were no 'wild' or 'domesticated' animals. No meat was eaten, and, as the welfare of all life was highly regarded, no animals were slain. The conscientious consideration of Nature maintained a superbly balanced environment, so that Nature reciprocated with an equitable climate through the year – so fertilisation, propagation, and harvesting were stages of a repetitive cycle that did not impose seasonal restrictions. All of the needs for a paradisal state of life were provided by Nature.

Being close to Nature, the spiritual faculties of humans were highly developed. Humanity was at peace and, being naturally spiritual, had due regard for everything in The Creation. Governments, judicial systems, civil laws and armed forces did not exist, for the need of them had not arisen. Humanity's spirituality ensured a consistently high level of proper behaviour. A lifetime spent on Earth was the opportunity for a Soul to develop its spirituality by familiarising itself with the physical laws of Nature during its practical experience of the reality of them. In so doing, the importance of the need to maintain the balance of the physical aspects of Nature was understood.

Procreation was the natural conclusion to the bond formed by the purest level of love generated by the total affinity between a man and a woman. Physical love play was only possible when the spiritual affinity between the genders was absolute. Physical attraction outside of the bond did not occur.

The social preoccupations were the quite minor tasks of gathering and preparing food. This was a pleasurable habit due to people's close affinity with Nature and their common participation in creative leisure activities, alongside the general development of their spiritual faculties.

It was an extremely healthy environment due to the compatible climate, a diet of natural foods, and the complete absence of stressful conditions. Occasional, accidentally acquired, physical ailments were treated with natural remedies and spiritual healing. Psychosomatic and stress-related disorders did not arise. Unexpected death was an unnatural event. It was understood that the immortal Soul only departed to its appointed Spiritrealm when the predestined physical experience on Earth had been completed. The departure of the Soul from Earthlife was a happy event, for it was understood that the Soul ascended into a higher state of being for eternity and the separation from those left behind was temporary. It was natural for spiritual contact to continue after the passage of the Soul into the Spiritrealms.

Any matters that required counselling or guidance were referred to Elders within the community or to higher entities in the Spiritrealms. There was no greed, no envy, no violence, no lust, no superiority or inferiority, for these are not spiritual traits.

The planet Earth – a physical creation of God – was maintained in divine order by the laws of Nature. Thus, the existence of spiritual Souls in physical bodies, in a physical habitat, necessitated conscientious adherence to and conformity with the laws. The spiritual Soul in its physical body was a guest in an environment that was alien to it. By complying with and adhering to the laws of Nature, Souls were performing the good service of The Creator, with The Creator.

George W. Gee

19

To see a World in a grain of sand
And a Heaven in a Wild Flower,
Hold Infinity in the palm of your hand
And Eternity in an Hour.
William Blake

And so, an energetic, curly-haired girl is walking through the lush, green land one day. Heaven – the earth's Soul – surrounds her in that tranquil oasis, and the animals that she passes graze unafraid. She has just fulfilled her daily communal duties, and so, she rests herself against a well. She inhales the sweet, fragranced air slowly and contentedly. Then, just for a second …

'Imagine how much more exhilarated I would feel if I could just lie here in the sun all day … if only someone else would fulfil my duties for me today. How much more wonderful this garden would seem if this happened!'

The freckled youth does not recognise any darkness in her thoughts. Darkness of thought is, in fact, alien to her. She just smiles innocently.

The girl now jumps high into the air in order to reach a branch directly above her. She, quite forcefully, plucks down a ripe apple.

She glares long and hard at it.

Staring.

For the first time in her life, she feels a new sensation: irritation.

She slowly begins to raise the apple towards her watering mouth.

Every cause has an effect.

(*Human innocence? Original sin?*)

'How tasty this apple would be, I am sure!' (*Poseidon begins to stir ... just for a moment.*) Suddenly, the youth hears William's familiar call far in the distance.

'I hear you, Father!' The words echo out from her mouth across the golden field – she knows that her father will *always* hear her, no matter what.

However, the girl remains statue-still for a few moments. She stares down at the apple once more, which still sits cosily in her hand. Affectionately, she begins to caress the glowing crimson fruit.

Suddenly she experiences a mysterious energy deep within herself.

'Follow your intuition,' whispers a clear, voice deep inside her heart.

In this instant, the girl has unknowingly discovered an immense secret: life is a process of creation – it is not a road of discovery. Life's grandest miracle is that the present is a gift: a blank canvas, on which to paint free choice.

All of a sudden, the youth declares: 'I have heard your voice and I will always follow you!'

Ocean-depth wisdom intermingles with the high tones of her bubbly voice.

And, it was in that very moment that individuals, who constituted a nation, began to make their own, unique choices, and they began to paint their own, unique canvases: a field of blossoming Souls is such a wonderful thing to behold, especially when the breeze of prior experience dances all around the flowers optimistically!

The little girl begins her run through the field joyously, zigzagging along the way.